Philip's life is in limbo. He can't leave the house where he was taken when he was rescued from Oscar, the man who raped him until he got pregnant with a boy. He isn't sure he wants to anyway. He and Myron are safe there, and for the first time in his life, he has friends, people who care for him. He even has a crush on Abel, one of the council members, but he knows nothing can come of it. Abel has his life in hand. He has an important job and no reason to be interested in Philip, not with the kind of baggage Philip comes with.

Abel has had a crush on Philip since the first time he saw him. He hasn't told him anything, because he knows it's not the right moment. Philip's son is only a few months old, and neither of them can leave the Bishop house. Abel can't help but hover close, though, helping with Myron when Philip needs him to — and falling deeper in love with him as the days pass.

The council is still torn in half, even now that Oscar is dead. The man who is going to choose his replacement, Alpha Grimes, is the same man who handed Philip off to Oscar, and that means nothing good can come out of his decision. But when Alpha Grimes dies, everything becomes possible again.

Family of the Heart
Copyright © 2019 Catherine Lievens
ISBN: 978-1-4874-2520-3
Cover art by Angela Waters

Published by eXtasy Books Inc or
Devine Destinies, an imprint of eXtasy Books Inc

Look for us online at:
www.eXtasybooks.com or www.devinedestinies.com

FAMILY OF THE HEART
ALLEGHENY SHIFTERS BOOK 4

BY

CATHERINE LIEVENS

CHAPTER ONE

Philip was doing his best not to stare, but Abel in a suit was hard to ignore. He wore it so well, and it was such a change from Abel's usually comfortable-looking clothes. It fascinated Philip, and it made him want to look even more than he normally did — which was already a lot.

At least he had something to focus on. He looked down and smiled at his son, cooing when Myron gave him a toothless smile. Myron caught Philip's finger and pulled it closer, no doubt to put it into his mouth.

"Do you want me to hold him for a bit so you can go dance?" Nico asked.

Philip shook his head. "I don't dance."

"So you can go to the bathroom, then."

"Thank you, but I'm fine."

"He meant so you can finally go talk to Abel," Nico's twin, Chris, intervened.

Philip wondered why he was sitting with them. He liked them, and most of the other carriers he was forced to live with, but sometimes they were a bit much. Maybe it was because Philip had been hidden and locked up most of his life, first by his family, then by the man who'd raped him and had killed his little girl before she even got a chance at life.

Philip swallowed. He couldn't think about that, especially not at a wedding celebration. Seamus and Alex deserved to see smiling faces around them, not Philip's horrified expression when he thought about his past. So Philip forced himself to smile. "Why should I want to talk to Abel?"

1

Calum snorted from the other side of the table, but he didn't say anything, and Philip was grateful for that. He was never sure how to talk to Calum, and he suspected he wasn't the only one. Calum spent most of his time in his room, and he was present tonight only because, well—Philip wasn't sure why. They hadn't been forced to attend the wedding. But Alex was a badger, and the badgers were the ones who'd offered Philip and the other carriers a safe place to stay while the council was hunting them to lock them up. Being there for Alex's wedding was a show of respect. Philip would have come just to make Seamus happy, though, and since Alex had been the one who'd rescued him from Oscar's claws, he had a special affection for him.

"Come on, Philip. Who are you trying to fool?" Chris asked.

Nico elbowed him in the ribs, but he didn't seem to care. Philip wasn't surprised. Chris was the next in line to become the alpha of his clowder, even though he was a carrier. He behaved like an alpha already, even though he was young and wouldn't take his father's place for years. He was used to people listening to him, and that hadn't changed just because he wasn't living with the clowder right now.

Philip shook his head and did his best to resist the urge to look at Abel again. "I don't know what you're talking about," he murmured.

"No? Well, I was talking about the fact that you always look at Abel like you're thirsty and he's the only one who has water."

Philip knew his cheeks were red. He could feel it.

"Or maybe *he's* the water," Nico mused.

Philip wanted to strangle them both. "It's not—I don't—"

He wasn't surprised when Nico reached for his arm and squeezed it. He was the sensitive twin, the one who always made sure no one got hurt by what he said or did. Chris cared, too, but he wasn't as soft and gentle as his twin. "You know we're just teasing, right?"

"Not about the way he looks at Abel," Chris said. "That shit's real, and everyone but Abel knows it."

Philips' stomach sank. "What?"

"Come on, Philip. We all have eyes, and the two of you have been dancing around each other ever since you arrived with him. He's been protective and shit, and we see the way he looks at you as well as the way *you* look at *him*."

Philip shook his head. "I'm sure you're wrong."

Chris arched a brow. "About you wanting to jump him?"

And there went Philips' cheeks again. "No." He supposed he might as well admit that. Like Chris and Nico were saying, it was obvious to most people, although Philip hoped it wasn't to Abel. He didn't know what he'd do if the man knew how he felt about him. "About him looking at me that way." Or any way.

A small commotion made the three of them look up. Several people, including Seamus, were heading inside the house. Philip wasn't sure why, but from who those people were, he could take a wild guess. They were no doubt going to talk about what was going on in the forest and how they could try dealing with the part of the council who thought carriers were nothing more than incubators for whoever paid them the most money.

"Abel's going with them," Nico noticed.

"He *is* a council member, you know," Chris said. "Even though he gets all soft and nice when he's with Philip." He turned back to Philip. "So? What's the problem? It's not that he's not your type, not when you look like you want to eat him up."

Goddammit. Couldn't they have stayed distracted? "He's a council member," Philip said quietly. "That means he needs someone he can take to whatever parties and dinners the

3

council has. He needs someone he can be proud to be seen with." And that could never be Philip. Not a lot of people knew what he'd been through, but the ones who did were enough. No one had ever judged him for it, for what had been done to him, but that didn't change the fact that it had tainted him.

He looked down at Myron. He loved his son with all his being, and he always would. That didn't change the way he was conceived, though. It didn't matter to Philip, but it would to other people, and no matter how gentle Abel was, he had to deal with those people. It was his job.

"Oh, no," Nico snapped.

That was so unusual for him that Philip blinked at him. "What?"

"You're not thinking what I think you're thinking, are you?"

"I have no idea. I can't read your mind."

Nico's eyes narrowed. "You *are* good enough. Abel *would* be proud to be seen with you. I know it. He's a good man."

"I know." Philip kept his gaze down. He didn't want to face Chris and Nico.

"Then what's the problem?"

"He wouldn't care, but what about everyone else?" And even knowing Abel didn't mind Philip's past, it was hard to believe he might want Philip the way Philip wanted him. Like Nico said, he was a good man, and that was probably the reason he was always so sweet and gentle. He knew what Philip had gone through and didn't want him to be hurt again. That was why he was so careful. It had to be.

"They can go fuck themselves," Chris said.

That startled a laugh out of Philip. "I'm not surprised that's what you think." After all, he was probably used to tongues wagging about him. He was the heir to his clowder, and he was a carrier. A carrier had never been an alpha.

Philip still wasn't sure it would happen, not with the way things were in the forest right now, but if there was anyone who could face the council and win this battle, it was Chris.

"It's not that simple," Philip tried to explain.

Chris snorted. "Yeah, it is. You want him, and he wants you. That's the only two people you need to think of. Well, and Myron, but he doesn't count since he doesn't have an opinion yet. He could do with a second dad, though, and so could you. You look like you're about to fall asleep on your plate."

Philip frowned. "That's because Myron still feeds at night."

"I know. I wasn't blaming you or anything. I just think it's stupid that you're letting what other people think stop you from being happy. I might be able to understand that if we were talking about your family, but we're not. The people who might have something to say about your relationship with Abel are assholes, so what do you care about then? Abel would be lucky to have you in his life like that. Being a carrier doesn't make you less of a person."

"I know that." But no matter what Chris thought, what other people would say *did* count. Abel's job with the council depended on it.

Oscar was dead.

Abel had never thought he'd hear those words. He didn't like Oscar—he hated him, and he suspected he wasn't the only one, albeit maybe not for the same reasons—but Oscar had been young, only in his mid-forties. He should have been a council member for another few decades.

Except he wouldn't be, and that was a good thing.

"Was it really an accident?" someone asked.

Abel shook himself. Oscar was dead, and that meant two

things—that the side of the council trying to do the right thing was one step closer to being able to overturn the carrier laws, and someone had probably killed Oscar.

Thomas snorted. "I don't think anyone believes it was. It would be too big a coincidence."

"Does that mean that one of us organized it, then?" Abel asked. He didn't care if the answer was yes, but he doubted it would be. Everyone looked stunned. They weren't all there, though. The wedding was a small affair, so most of the alphas and the council members they were working with weren't present. It could be one of them. It also could be anyone else in the forest, though. Oscar had been an asshole, and everyone shared that opinion.

Thomas leaned back in his chair. "I don't know. Did you?"

"Of course not." Although Abel wished he had. He'd wanted Oscar to pay for what he'd done to Philip. He had, but not because Abel had done anything about it.

"We didn't do anything either, and I don't need Morris to tell us the bears haven't."

"It could be one of the other alphas or council members."

"We'll need to ask them about it."

Abel doubted anyone would admit to having done it, and he wasn't sure they'd be lying. "A lot of people hated Oscar."

"I agree. It would be best if we found out who was behind this, though. I'm not planning on handing them over to the police, but I'd like to know who we need to thank."

Abel should have been outraged at Thomas' suggestion that even if they did find out who was behind this, they wouldn't denounce them. He wasn't. He might have been a few years ago, but he'd seen too much since then. Some alphas and council members used their power and their position to kidnap and torture people, mainly carriers, who should be cherished. They deserved everything they got, and Abel didn't care how it happened. If he hadn't been afraid of losing everything, including Philip, he might have gone after Oscar himself.

"We should go back to the party," Alex said. "I doubt we can find out anything tonight."

"I'll stay here and make some calls," his father said. He and Thomas were close, and Abel could see Alex wanted to tell him to leave it for tonight.

"Why don't we all go back, and Morris and I can help you text the people who should know about this?" he suggested. "It's your son's wedding. You should be having fun."

"Especially since I'm your last kid to get married," Alex pointed out with a smile.

"Alex is right. Staying behind to make phone calls isn't going to change the fact that we can't do much tonight. Besides, I'm sure most of the council members already know about this. This kind of news has a way of getting around. I'll send a mass text. I'm sure we'll have a meeting tomorrow anyway." He wasn't looking forward to it, but the council needed to regroup. Abel especially needed to talk to the members on his side, but it could wait for a few hours.

They headed back to the party. Some people seemed to have noticed they'd been gone for a while, although that was probably because Alex and Seamus had been with them. A wedding party without the grooms was weird.

Philip was still at the table with Chris and Nico. There were others with them, but as always, Philip was focusing on Myron. He was a great dad and a good man, and he didn't deserve what had been done to him. He was brave and strong, and he should have all the happiness he hadn't had in the first part of his life.

Abel wasn't sure how to make sure he got that, though. He wanted to help, and more than anything, he wanted to be part of Philip's life. He knew it wasn't a good idea, and he'd stayed away.

Philip had been raped and tortured by a council member, someone who had power over him. Abel didn't, not the same way Oscar had, since both he and Philip were porcupine shifters, but that didn't change the fact that he *was* a council member. He didn't want to put Philip in the position of possibly agreeing to be with him just because of that. He didn't know how Philip was, what he thought of when they talked, how he saw him. He wasn't sure he wanted to know.

Or maybe he did. He could admit he had a crush on Philip, at least to himself. How could he not be half in love with him? He wasn't only beautiful—he was everything Abel could want in a man. He lit up the room when he was there, with his quiet strength and the obvious love for his son.

Abel didn't want to risk changing Philip's life again, not when he'd just found a new balance. Philip deserved the best, and Abel was pretty sure that wasn't him. He could give Philip a lot—his love, a home, a co-parent for Myron, a comfortable life—but Philip could find that with a lot of other people.

Abel was a deer shifter, not a predator. Some people thought that made him weak. He also wasn't the best looking man. He was okay, he supposed, maybe even cute—or so he'd been told—but Philip could have someone gorgeous, just like he was. Of course, looks weren't everything, but that still didn't mean Abel deserved Philip, or that Philip would ever want him the way he wanted him.

But he could be a friend to him. He could be there if Philip needed him. Philip had a lot of friends, but surely he could do with one more?

Abel was hesitant, but he forced himself to walk toward the table where Philip and the other carriers were sitting. The twins were with him, but they both looked up as one when Abel was almost there. It was freaky, but Abel just smiled at them. One of them—possibly Nico, but Abel wouldn't have sworn it—smiled, then grabbed the other's hand and pulled him toward the dance floor. Abel didn't miss the way the other twin—it had to be Chris—looked at one of the men in uniform that lined the sides of the room for protection.

But Abel's attention didn't stay on the twins. It went back to Philip, just like always when Philip was anywhere close.

"Can I sit here?" Abel asked.

Philip's cheeks flushed. "Of course."

"Thank you."

"You're always welcome at my table, Abel."

Abel hoped he wasn't blushing. That was adorable on Philip, but it probably made Abel look like he'd just run a marathon. "Thank you." He sat on the chair closest to Philip.

They were silent for a bit, and Abel stared at Philip in what he hoped wasn't an obvious way. Philip was looking at the dancefloor, and more specifically, at Alex and Seamus. They were slow dancing, even though the song was a fast one and everyone else was bouncing around them. Seamus probably wouldn't have been able to do that, but Abel doubted that was the reason he and Alex were pressed against each other. He was going on being seven months pregnant, and he'd just married the love of his life.

Abel cleared his throat. "Do you want me to hold Myron for a bit? You could go dance with your friends." Or with whatever man caught his attention. Abel hoped that wouldn't happen, but he wouldn't say anything about it if it did. It wasn't his business, and he didn't have a say in who Philip talked and danced with.

Philip shook his head. "I'm fine. Thank you."

Abel wanted to ask Philip if he wanted to dance, but he didn't think he'd get a different answer, so he didn't.

"God, you two are so boring," Chris said. He reached for Myron, and Abel was only mildly surprised when Philip handed his son over without saying anything. He trusted Chris and the other carriers they lived with. Except maybe Calum, but that was more because Calum kept so much to himself that no one really knew him.

"I'm going to take this little guy for a spin on the dance floor," Chris said. "You two should do the same. Abel, ask him, because he's never going to take the initiative." With that, Chris was off, leaving Abel and Philip alone and his words heavy in the air around them.

Philip wanted to hit Chris right now, or maybe to tickle him or whatever. Chris was already gone, though, and Philip followed him with his gaze, smiling when he realized Chris was *really* going to dance with Myron. It was ridiculous, but also adorable, and Philip wasn't the only one noticing that. Jacob, one of the guards that lived with them at the Bishop house and made sure they were protected, couldn't seem to look away from Chris.

"Do you think he'll come back to bug us if we don't obey his order?" Abel asked.

Philip swallowed. He wanted to dance with Abel, but he didn't want Abel to feel like he had to ask him just because Chris had mentioned it. "You don't have to do it. I mean, it's just Chris and his ideas, you know. Sometimes, he already acts like the alpha he will be, and he doesn't realize we're not his clowder members."

Abel hesitated, and Philip was surprised at his next words. "What if I want to ask you to dance?"

"You do?"

Abel got up and leaned toward Philip, offering him his hand. "Will you do me the honor of dancing with me?"

Philip knew he was blushing. He couldn't seem to help it. He took Abel's hand, though, because how could he not? This was something he'd wanted ever since Abel had helped him the first time—hell, since he'd first seen Abel. Philip had been terrified, but even then, he'd been able to see that Abel had a gentle soul and that he would never hurt him. He still believed that. Everything Abel had said or done told Philip he was the good man he appeared to be.

And Philip wanted him in his life.

He wasn't foolish enough to think that there would ever be anything between them. Abel could have much better than Philip, and he deserved it. He *needed* someone better because of his position as a council member. Philip could have this night, though. This dance.

He let Abel pull him to his feet and guide him toward the dance floor. His cheeks felt hot, especially because of the stares he could feel on them. A lot of people had teased about the way he kept staring at Abel and about how much time they spent together when Abel happened to be at the Bishop house. They were probably curious, wondering if the fact that they were going to dance together meant there *was* something between them. Philip was going to have to answer so many questions later tonight when he and the others went home. He wasn't looking forward to it, but maybe it would be worth it, worth feeling Abel's arms around him.

The song shifted to a slow one just as they stepped onto the dance floor. Philip swallowed. Was Abel going to change his mind?

He didn't. He moved in front of Philip and opened his arms, and Philip went right into them. It was a bit weird— the last time he'd been this close to someone, it had been Oscar, and he'd been raped. Philip almost expected to be afraid, but he wasn't, not when Abel was so careful with him.

11

Abel wrapped his arms around Philip, keeping them loose, no doubt so Philip could get away if he needed to.

Philip didn't, though. He wanted to stay right there for-ever. He leaned closer, smiling at the scent of Abel's cologne.

"I think you should be the one leading," Abel said softly.

"Why?"

"You're taller."

Philip chuckled. "That doesn't mean I know how to dance. This is my first time."

Abel grinned. "It's mine, too."

"It is? I would have thought you'd have done this plenty of times."

"I haven't. I wasn't very popular when I was a teenager. No one wanted to dance with me, and thank God, because I'd probably have stepped on their toes and made both of us stumble."

"You're doing well." They were both a bit clumsy and tense, and Philip wasn't sure if it was because they didn't know what they were doing or because of the stares.

"You are, too. I feel a bit like we're on display, though."

So it *was* the stares. "I'm sorry. Chris shouldn't have pushed you to ask me to dance. I know how you hate being at the center of attention."

"You're right, I do, but I think it's worth it."

Philip blinked. "It is?"

"Yes. I like dancing with you. I think we fit together well, don't you?"

He was talking about dancing. That was all. Philip had to remember that. "We do." They weren't doing much more than holding each other and moving in circles, but at least they weren't tripping each other.

He leaned closer. Abel was warm, and he was making Philip feel that way, too. His arms were wrapped around Philip's waist, and he was smiling. Philip found himself smiling back.

He liked this. He liked being in Abel's arms. He wanted to spend more time there, but when the song ended, he took a step back.

Abel frowned. "Do you want to get back to Myron?"

Philip loved his son, but right now, he wanted to stay with Abel, to have a little time with him. He didn't like that he felt that way, but he'd spent nearly every second of every day with Myron since his birth. He wasn't just a dad, even though that was his main persona right now. He was also a man. A man who'd been brutalized, but still a man, and he wanted love.

He looked around to find Chris and Myron. They weren't dancing anymore. Chris was standing by Jacob, talking to him. He looked up, and his gaze crossed Philip's. Philip moved toward him, but Chris shook his head and tilted his chin at Abel in a clear order.

Philip scowled at him. He wasn't a bobcat shifter, and even if he were, Chris wasn't an alpha yet. He couldn't order him around.

But was it an order if Philip wanted that, too? Myron was safe with Chris. For all that Chris could be forceful, he'd keep Myron safe. Besides, there were plenty of people around who would do that if something happened. Philip was with friends. He was protected, as were the other carriers. They weren't at the Bishop house, but they were in cete territory, and that meant that no one could touch them, not with the number of guards keeping an eye on things.

"I think he wants us to keep dancing," Abel said. He sounded amused, and Philip could admit the situation *was* kind of funny. He also wanted to take this chance, because when would he have one like this again? All the sons of the badger alpha were married now. The carriers couldn't travel from one territory to another, not when the council law that said they should be handed over was still in place.

The next song was another slow one. Alex and Seamus were still dancing, lost in each other, and the person in charge of the music was humoring them. Plenty of other people were dancing, too, and Philip stepped toward Abel again.

This time, he was the one who reached out, even though he was blushing like crazy. "We should do what Chris wants us to do. It'll make him happy to have someone listen to him for once."

"You're feeding his alpha tendencies."

"So? He's going to take his father's place sooner or later."

"Maybe."

They both knew the future was still uncertain, and that while there wasn't a law that forbade carriers from becoming alphas, one might be put in place next week, or next month. Neither of them said anything about it, though.

Abel stepped into Philip's arms again. They started swaying to the sound of the music, and Philip closed his eyes. Abel was in his arms, around him, surrounding him and making him feel safer than he'd ever felt. He could forget about the clusterfuck that his life was for a bit, just the time of one last dance.

His problems would still be there when it was over and he was alone again. He'd still be a single father. His life would still be in danger.

He'd still love his son. He'd still be half in love with Abel. He'd still think nothing could happen between them.

But for the time of a song, he could fake it and imagine that he and Abel were in love and happy together.

Abel never wanted to let go. He was going to have to find a present for Chris to thank him for giving him this chance of being close to Philip. It felt so good to be there, in his arms. It was a bit like a dream, and while Abel knew he was going to have to wake up eventually, he didn't want to.

It was Myron that broke the spell. His cries jolted Abel out of the dream, and when he opened his eyes, he realized that Philip's attention was already on his son. He didn't berate him for it. Hell, he wanted to check in on Myron too. That didn't mean he wouldn't miss what they'd had for a few minutes.

Abel stepped away. "Go check in on him. I'm sure Chris will want his turn to dance with an adult."

Philip smiled. "Maybe Jacob."

"Maybe." That situation was complicated, though, and Abel was glad he wasn't in the middle of it.

Philip shuffled. "Why don't you come with me? We can sit together. I don't know what Myron's problem is, but it shouldn't be hard to solve. He probably needs to be changed."

"I can do that."

Philip shook his head. "I'll do it, but thanks. You could go sit down. I'll be right back."

Abel watched him walk away. He had to pull his gaze up, because it drifted down of its own volition. He was pretty sure a few of the carriers had noticed him from their smirks, but thank God Chris was busy talking with Philip and handing him Myron, so he wouldn't tease Abel.

Abel went back to the table where Philip had been sitting earlier. Calum was gone, probably pouting in a corner, or maybe bribing someone to take him back to the Bishop house. Who knew with him?

Abel settled in his chair and waited. His hands still tingled from the contact with Philip. They'd never been that close, and Abel wasn't sure they'd get another opportunity. He could ask, no doubt, but what would Philip say? He hadn't seemed bothered by the closeness, but they'd been dancing in a public place. Maybe he hadn't wanted to cause problems or something.

Or maybe he hadn't minded but wouldn't want to do anything like this again because they were only friends. Abel could deal with that if it meant making Philip happy.

"Here we are."

Abel looked up. Philip slid into his chair, a drowsy Myron in his arms. "That was fast."

"I've gotten good at this."

"You have. You're a great father."

Philip's cheeks flushed. "Thank you." He was silent for a moment, and Abel settled in to watch the people still on the dance floor.

Then Philip said, "I wasn't sure, you know."

"You weren't sure about what?" Abel kept his voice quiet, gentle. He could tell that whatever Philip wanted to tell him wasn't easy, and he didn't want to spook him or to make him change his mind. He wanted to know everything there was to know about Philip, the good and the bad, even the ugly.

"That I should keep him. I love him. I've loved him since I realized I was pregnant with him. But I'll never be able to forget how he was conceived, and whose son he is. I don't care about any of that. I know not everyone will pass over that, though."

"Not a lot of people know he's Oscar's son."

Philip shook his head. "He's not, not really."

"You're right. He's *your* son, and like I said, you're doing a great job. He's going to grow up a nice, loving man, and it will all be thanks to you."

"Thomas told me that if I wanted, he could find a family for Myron. It wouldn't have been hard, since he's the alpha. I knew it would have been a good family, and it was tempting." He cuddled Myron close. "But I couldn't do it. Even though I wasn't sure I could be a good father, or that I could forget how he came to be. I love him."

"As it should be. I don't think anyone looks at Myron and thinks about how he was conceived. They think of you and how strong you are, that you're a great father and that Myron couldn't want for anything else. He's lucky to have you, Philip." Anyone would be, but Abel didn't say that out loud. Now wasn't the time to hint about that, not when Philip was focused on his son.

The moment slid away. Abel had done what he could to reassure Philip, and he hoped it had worked. He knew that he could repeat the same things again and again and that they wouldn't help until Philip accepted them and believed them. Sometimes people could be their own worst enemy. Abel was guilty of that, too, and he knew how hard it was to be positive and see things objectively.

"They're having fun," Philip murmured.

Everyone was. Abel and Philip might be sitting at the table, and Calum might be gone, but everyone else was still there, most of them on the dance floor. Chris had convinced Jacob to dance with him, even though Jacob kept peeking at his alpha. Seamus and Alex were on the side of the room, quietly talking. Alex's brothers were dancing with their husbands, and even the other carriers were right there. They were close together, as if they were wary of the other people, but as time passed, Abel saw them visibly relax. It was a good thing. They all deserved to have fun and be happy. Some of them had been treated well by their alphas and their people, but some, like Josiah, had gone through hell.

They were safe now. Even with Jacob awkwardly dancing with Chris, there were plenty of guards to make sure nothing happened. It might be their last celebration for a while, especially with Oscar being dead. No one could tell what would happen next, and they all should take advantage of this time of reprieve.

"Thank you," Philip said without looking away from the dance floor.

"What for?"

"For the dance. Having a moment to myself was nice. I love Myron, but sometimes, I feel like I'm only a dad."

"Any time. I can take care of Myron if you need some time off. I might not be a father, but I understand feeling like only part of who you are is important. Sometimes it feels like everyone only cares that I'm a council member. The job doesn't leave me a lot of time to be myself."

Philip looked at Abel. "You can always be yourself with me."

"I know." And he did. Philip was one of the few people who Abel felt could see *him* rather than the council member. He was both, of course, but not one part of him was more important than the other. Not everyone realized that.

Philip did.

Chapter Two

The knock on the door was a welcome distraction. Abel glared at the files he should have been reading but wasn't because he couldn't stop thinking about Philip and called out, "Come in!"

The door opened, and his sister's head peeked through. Abel smiled and relaxed. He'd half expected it to be yet another council member, or maybe Alpha Rod Garrison who wanted an update Abel didn't have. As far as he knew, no one had an update on what had happened to Oscar, and asking every ten minutes wasn't going to change that. The only thing it *was* doing was driving Abel crazy, even though he understood why people were anxious. *He* was anxious, and he was right in the middle of things.

"Am I disturbing you?" Allison asked.

Abel leaned back in his chair. "No. Come on. Distract me from the cluster fuck that is my job right now."

She smiled. "The Oscar thing, huh?"

"Yeah." Abel hadn't told her or anyone else the details, but the news had spread like wildfire in the forest. Oscar, a notorious asshole and bad man, had died in a car accident that might not have been an accident. Abel was ready to bet he wasn't the only council member being hounded for answers. The problem was that he didn't have them yet.

"How was the party the other night?"

Abel smiled. The thought of dancing with Philip was enough to make him forget about Oscar, at least for a while. "It was good. Seamus and Alex are happy, and they belong together."

"Did you talk to Camden?"

Camden was Allison's son, and he'd been kidnapped and held by Oscar, along with Philip. Camden hadn't been in Oscars' hands for long, but his fate would have been similar to Philip's if he had. Abel owed the cete a lot for rescuing him before it could happen. "Yes. He's doing fine. Grumbling because he's stuck there, but he knows it's better than what would happen to him if he came home. Besides, he's not alone. Vincent is keeping him tranquil."

Her shoulders' relaxed. "Thank God. I wish he could come home, too, but as long as that law holds up . . ."

Abel sighed and rubbed his face. He wanted to tell his sister that the carrier law would be stricken down soon, but he couldn't. He didn't want to lie to her. "We're one step closer to making it happen, but you know how it works. The porcupine alpha is going to have to elect a new council member for the prickle, and no one but him has a say in who it will be."

"Do you think he'll choose a good person this time?"

Again, Abel wanted to say yes, but he couldn't. "He's not an easy man to deal with." And he'd been right there with Oscar when it came to the way they treated carriers. Abel had talked to Camden and Vincent, and he knew that Oscar and Alpha Grimes had planned to keep them. Vincent had been crying when he'd said that Alpha Grimes had liked him and was going to get him pregnant.

Abel tightened his hands into fists. He wished he could pound both Alpha Grimes and Oscar into the ground. Of course, Alpha Grimes could probably beat him easily. He wasn't a fighter. Some days, he wasn't even sure why he'd been chosen as the herd's council member. "It's not going to be easy."

Allison nodded. "I realize that. And at least Camden and

Vincent are safe."

"They are. The cete will make sure nothing happens to them. They're good people."

She smiled, albeit a little sadly. "You wouldn't be friends with them if they weren't. I'm just worried about my son."

"I know." And Abel shared that worry. Camden and Vincent were safe, and they would be for as long as the cete and the sleuth held their ground. That didn't mean their lives were great, though. They shared a large and pretty house with people who'd become friends to them, they were fed and entertained, and they were even homeschooled, but that didn't change the fact that they were under house arrest. They couldn't leave the Bishop house, and when they did— which wasn't often because it was too dangerous—they had to stick to cete territory. Of course, they could shift and run in the forest since the house was isolated, but Abel suspected that only helped so much for some of the carriers. "I can call the house."

Allison's eyes widened. "You can?"

Even the phone calls had to be kept at a minimum in case someone suspected something. They couldn't afford for the wrong people to think they were hiding the carriers. But Abel could do this for his sister. He knew how much she missed Camden. She'd barely had the chance to see him after Alex took him to the Bishop house.

Abel grabbed his phone and dialed the number of one of the guards. Things had been set up so that he'd pass on the phone to the person who was receiving the call. They couldn't do it often, but it was a way to make both Allison and Camden happy, and Abel needed some of that happiness in his life.

Allison's eyes glittered with tears as she took it. Abel wished he could do more, but he was waiting, just like the other council members were. They needed to know what

Alpha Grimes had up his sleeve before they took the next step. It was impossible to plan without knowing what he'd do.

Allison left his office in tears when she was done with her call. Abel made a mental note to visit Camden as soon as he could. The fact that Philip lived in the same house gave him even more of an incentive to make the trip, even though it would take him a few hours. Maybe he could stop at Thomas' house and talk to him too.

His phone chirped, and he groaned. He recognized the sound. It was the one he'd assigned to the other council members, so this could be either good or bad. Either way, it wasn't going to be fun.

The text was from the council's secretary. There was another meeting planned tomorrow, as if the one they'd had the day after Oscar had died hadn't been enough. Abel doubted there was news, not yet, but it wasn't like he could decline.

He sighed again and dialed Calder's number. Calder was the badger council member, and one of Abel's closest friends. "You got the text?" Abel asked as soon as Calder answered.

"Yeah. I'm not looking forward to this."

"Neither am I. How loud do you think Jacqueline and the others are going to get?"

"Too loud. Do you think anyone knows something more than last time? Because I don't, and I don't see the need for another meeting."

"I doubt it. We're probably meeting so Jacqueline can rant about how no one is doing anything."

"Maybe she was in love with Oscar. I mean, we worked with the man for years and we don't care what happened to him. I don't see why she does."

Abel grimaced. He did *not* need to think about Jacqueline

and Oscar together. "I don't know. We should probably try to find out what this meeting is about."

"How about we meet at the Bishop house? That way you can check in on your nephew and on your man, and we can talk about it face to face. I'll text the others and see if any of them can come."

Abel closed his eyes. Of course Calder had noticed his interest with Philip. Was there anyone who hadn't? Hopefully, Philip, but Abel wasn't too sure about that anymore. He'd never thought he was this transparent. "It will be good to visit Camden."

"I see we're not talking about Philip. That's fine. I can corner you later, maybe after watching the two of you together. You're adorable, both of you. I always want to push your heads together and make you kiss."

"I hate you."

"And hate is close to love. So you love me."

"Why did Thomas pick you as a council member again? Because you sound like you could be my nephew's best friend, and he's not even eighteen yet."

"I'm one of those guys who always stays young."

"Ah, you mean you're a Peter Pan. You don't want to grow up."

"I wouldn't be the cete's council member if I couldn't behave like an adult sometimes. I don't see why I should do it all the time, though."

Abel shook his head. It was always good to talk to Calder. "I'll see you tonight at the house?"

"Yep. But maybe you should head there right now. It would give more time to spend with Philip."

Abel didn't want to admit it, but he was going to do just that.

Philip always seemed to have a smile on his face when he was with the other carriers. Sometimes, it was hard for him to believe he had friends, but he did. He couldn't deny it, and he didn't want to. He wasn't alone in the world any-more—alone against a monster bent on hurting him.

He had a family now, and not just Myron. He knew that even when they were all able to go home, wherever that home was, they'd keep in touch. Well, except maybe with Calum, but that was more because Calum still kept to himself than because Philip and the others didn't care about him. It was hard to care for someone who didn't talk to you, though.

"So, what's going on with you and Abel?" Redley asked. The fox shifter was smirking, and Philip suspected he knew *exactly* what was going on.

Philip checked on Myron, who was on a blanket on the floor trying to roll from his back to his stomach, but he couldn't use his son as a reason to avoid answering for long. "Nothing. We're friends, I guess."

"That dance the other night looked like more than friends to me."

"It wasn't. We were just having fun."

"You could have fun of the naked variety with him if you wanted to," Chris said. He was sucking on a lollipop, his feet hanging off the side of the armchair he was spread in. He was watching TV, or at least that was what Philip had thought.

"We're just friends," Philip insisted. He wasn't going to veer off that answer. He and Abel *were* friends, or at least he hoped so. They weren't spending a lot of time together, though, so who knew? Maybe Philip thought they were friends, but Abel didn't. It wasn't like they'd talked about it. It was true that Abel was always gentle with Philip and My-ron, but that was just the kind of man he was.

Chris flopped around until he faced Philip. "But is that all you want from him? Forget about what's going on between you and what you have. Do you want more?"

Philip didn't want to answer that question. "What about you and Jacob? What's going on with you?"

Chris grimaced. "Way to change the subject, Philip. And I'm not answering any questions on that."

Philip arched a brow. "Why should I answer your questions about Abel and me, then?"

Chris laughed. "You got me. I'm dying to know, but I'll stop asking questions. I guess I have more than enough to deal with anyway."

Now Philip felt guilty about bringing Jacob up, especially with others around them. Redley was the only one paying attention to the conversation, and Nico probably already knew about whatever Chris was hiding, and Hector and Kaspar's attention were on the TV, but that didn't mean they hadn't heard. Still, he wanted Chris to know he had someone else to talk to if he didn't want to talk to Nico. Sometimes being family made it harder, or at least Philip supposed it did. He didn't exactly have any experience when it came to that.

He swallowed. He didn't want to make Chris angry, but he wanted him to know. "If you ever need to talk . . ."

Chris shrugged. "There isn't much to talk about. Jacob's the one who has a problem."

"So you don't? I mean, about being both a carrier and your father's heir?" It was something that fascinated Philip. He knew that being a carrier didn't make him or Chris less than other people who weren't, but then, he wasn't next in line to become an alpha. He knew how hard people could be on carriers, and the fact that he was one would make things harder on Chris.

"Why should I? Being a carrier doesn't mean I can't be in

charge. So I'm going to get pregnant one day. What's the problem with that?"

"I don't have a problem with it, and neither does anyone here. I was just curious."

Chris grinned. "I'm not angry or offended. And I know you guys, of all people, can understand me. You know what it feels like to be a carrier, even though none of you is going to be an alpha." He winked. "You might become a council member's husband, though. That would be nice."

Philip flushed. "I told you, we're just friends. Besides, won't the council decide who I'm going to marry?" It was the way things had always worked. Philip was twenty-eight, and that meant he was too old to choose for himself. He hadn't been able to choose before, not when Oscar had kept him prisoner, and now it was too late.

Chris' eyes bugged. "The council? Are you serious? They're the guys we're running from."

"Yeah, but they're still the ones in charge."

"But our guys are going to win. I mean, that's why we're here, right? Why they're trying to have someone good elected as the next porcupine council member. They want to make things right, and that means also taking out that stupid twenty-six-year-old rule. You're going to be able to choose whoever you want to be with. We all are."

Philip leaned harder against the back of the couch. What Chris was saying made sense. The council members who were on their side were working hard, as were the alphas. They wanted things to change. Philip hadn't allowed himself to think about what would come next once the carriers were free and left the Bishop house. He knew it was stupid to think he might be allowed to stay. He was a porcupine, and this was cete territory. The only way he could stay would be to marry a badger, but Abel was a deer.

Of course, it wasn't like Philip was going to marry Abel.

But what was he going to do? Go back to the prickle and the people who had turned a blind eye on what Oscar did to him? Go back to the alpha who'd put him in Oscar's hands to begin with and who was going to rape a kid to get what he wanted? Or he could move to Northwood. The town was shared by all the different shifters in the forest. He could stay there, but he didn't have a job, and he didn't know what he could do. He'd never been allowed to go to school. He'd been homeschooled, so he could read and write, but was that enough to get a job? And what would he do with Myron? The thought of putting him in daycare was terrifying. Philip knew he'd need to spend some time away from his son sooner or later, but after what Oscar had done to his daughter, he didn't want to.

"I know it's hard to wrap your mind around all this," Chris said, his voice more serious. "It is for me, too. I was always told I had to hide what I was because no one would take me seriously if they knew. But my dad doesn't have other male kids. It's just Nico and me, and we're both carriers. Dad wants me to take his place, and he says there's enough time for things to change before he has to step down. I trust him, and I trust the other people working for things to change. It's time. I'm not saying it's going to be easy, but it has to be done, and we're stronger than people give us credit for. I mean, look at you and what you've gone through. You're still standing, and you're still living. You deserve to be able to choose what and who you want in the future."

Philip focused on Myron. The conversation was making him uncomfortable. He knew it was partly because he hated even thinking about the time he'd spent with Oscar, but it was more than that. He'd always been told he had to do what others decided for him, Alpha Grimes first, Oscar next. His own parents had hammered that into him, and they hadn't tried to stop Alpha Grimes when he'd taken him.

This world was different, though. Chris was right—a lot of people were working to make things better for him and the other carriers. If they managed, Philip would have a choice for the first time in his life.

That thought was petrifying. He didn't know how to choose for himself, let alone for his son. What if he fucked up?

"Do we know anything more about the car accident that killed Oscar?" Morris asked.

He and some of their group were in the Bishop house's kitchen. Some of the carriers had grumbled because they had to get dinner ready, so Thomas had sent someone to grab pizzas. It would be nice for the carriers, because they didn't often have the opportunity to have take-out, and it gave Abel and the others time to talk about what was going on.

"I haven't been able to find out anything," Calder said. "But the council is meeting tomorrow, so we might know more then."

"Do we know who might replace Oscar?"

"There's no way to know. Alpha Grimes is going to be the one choosing, and he's not a friend of ours."

That was an understatement. Abel wanted to get his hands on the man every time he thought about him, One of Philip's jailers was dead, but the other was still in charge of the prickle, and God only knew who else had had a hand in what was done to Philip. Abel had never asked Philip, but he always wondered about his parents. Why hadn't they tried to get Philip away from Grimes and Oscar? Or had they? Maybe they'd been punished for it. Abel had no way to know. Grimes was secretive when it came to his prickle. A lot of other alphas were, but now they knew Grimes was up to no good. The problem was that they couldn't stop him.

Alphas had absolute power over their members as long as they followed the laws put in place by the council. Oscar might be dead, but Abel had no doubt that he hadn't been the only council member backing Grimes and whatever he was doing.

So they didn't have a way to find out who Grimes was going to select. They didn't know Grimes well enough to take a guess.

They knew someone who might, though.

Abel hated the thought that had popped into his mind, but it might be worth exploring. He cleared his throat and waited until he had everyone's attention. "The point here is that we need someone who knows Grimes and who can take a wild guess at who the man is going to select. That means that someone needs to know the way the prickle works." Abel hated his next words. "We have a porcupine shifter here. Philip might know."

There was a pause before Thomas asked," Are you sure we should ask him? I know he's strong and that he's been doing incredibly well here, but he's still fragile."

Abel sighed. "I know, and trust me, if there were another way, I'd choose that. But we need insights on the prickle, and he's the only one who can give that to us. I'm not going to force him or anything. I'll ask him if he feels okay to talk about it, and if he says no, then that's it. But he might be our only way to be able to foresee what Grimes might do and plan for it."

"We should give Philip a chance," Calder agreed.

Abel relaxed. He still didn't like it, but the fact that he wasn't the only one thinking it was worth a try helped.

Thomas looked as reluctant as Abel felt, but he nodded. "All right. You should go find him, Abel."

Abel blinked. "Right now?" He knew why Thomas

thought he should be the one to talk to Philip, but he'd thought he'd have some time to get ready for it, maybe to think of a way to ask Philip.

"Why not? We're here. Philip is here. You two are friends, right? You can try talking to him. Besides, the sooner we have answers, the better it will be for everyone. We *need* to know what Grimes is planning. This is the one occasion we have to shift the balance of the council, and we all know what's going to happen if Grimes picks another Oscar."

Abel rubbed his forehead. He did know what would happen, and Thomas was right. This *was* their only chance. They had to do whatever it took to make sure the balance shifted their way, and Abel had no idea how they were going to do that. Alpha Grimes was the only one who could appoint the prickle's next council member. If they couldn't influence him, they'd have to get rid of him somehow.

Talking to Philip was the first step, but this situation was going to become more complicated before it got solved, however that happened.

"I'll go." Abel didn't want to. He didn't want to hurt Philip and to force him to think about his past. But if they didn't do this, Philip would be hurt even more, and that wasn't something Abel could allow.

He'd noticed Philip in the living room with some of the other carriers earlier, so he headed that way. He paused at the living room door and watched then, smiling at the sight of Philip being relaxed and talking to his friends. He didn't want to break that, but waiting wouldn't make things easier.

He knocked on the door. "Philip? Can I talk to you for a second?"

Chris wiggled his eyebrows. "Oh, that sounds good. Go on, Philip. We'll keep an eye on Myron."

Philip's cheeks were flushed as he got up from the couch and walked toward Abel. Abel wished he had something else to tell him, something that wouldn't wipe the smile right off his face.

They moved to the entrance. Abel shuffled, trying to find a way to tell Philip what he needed without spooking him. "You know we're having a meeting right now."

Philip frowned. "I do. I saw you and the others come in, and Kaspar has been grumbling about not being allowed in the kitchen."

"We're discussing Oscar and Grimes. We need to know who the best person would be to take Oscar's place and who Grimes will probably pick instead." Abel swallowed. "You're the only one who can give us an idea of that. You're the only one who's lived there and who knows the prickle well enough to give us answers. I'd like you to talk to me and the others about it, if you're okay with it. You don't have to if you're uncomfortable, but it would help us. We need to have at least an idea of what Grimes is planning so we can counter-plan him."

"I don't know anything."

Abel nodded. "That's okay. But you do know Grimes."

"Because he's my alpha."

"Not anymore, Philip. You won't have to see him ever again if you don't want to, I promise. But you know him, and you might be able to tell us what he's planning. Who do you think he'll choose as the next council member?"

Philip shook his head. "I don't know anything. I can't— why do you think I can help you? I'm just a guy who was brutalized. I don't—"

Abel raised his hands. "It's fine. Like I said, you don't have to do anything if you don't want to." Abel should have known this wasn't going to end well. Now he'd scared Philip and had possibly pushed him away, which was the last thing he'd wanted to do.

"I just don't understand why you and the other council

members want to hear from me. You know what I am and what happened to me. What I think isn't important."

This wasn't what Abel had expected. "Of course it is. You might not have chosen it, but you spent a lot of time with Oscar, and you grew up with Grimes." Abel reached out, hoping not to freak Philip out even more than he already was. "Everyone in the kitchen is safe. They're not going to hurt you or judge you. We all know what happened, and while I know how hard it's going to be for you, we're not going to talk about that. We want your insight on who would be the best council member so that the council can get rid of that horrible carrier law and who you think Grimes is going to choose. That's all. I'll be there with you the entire time, and you can leave whenever you want."

Abel wasn't sure that would help Philip feel better, but it didn't change the fact that he'd do everything he'd just mentioned. He'd be there for Philip. Philip deserved that, and so much more.

Philip wasn't sure what to say to Abel. He knew the people in the kitchen wouldn't hurt him. No one in the Bishop house would. But he was stunned.

No one had ever wanted his opinion before. He'd always obeyed orders, decisions that had been made without asking him what he thought about it. And now Abel wanted him to have an opinion on something this important? What if he fucked things up? What if he told them what he thought, and it was the wrong thing? The wrong person?

Because he knew who *he'd* select as the prickle's council member if he had a say in it. His choice could be wrong, though. He hadn't lived with the prickle in years, even though he'd still been in prickle territory. He'd been isolated by Oscar and Alpha Grimes, and things could have changed during that time. They ought to have. *He'd* changed.

"You don't have to come," Abel said. His voice was soft and soothing.

That made Philip realize he *had* to do this. What if he didn't, and everything got messed up because of it? What if Alpha Grimes chose someone worse than Oscar? Philip shook his head. "I'll come. I don't know how much help I can give you, but I'll do my best."

Abel's smile was gentle. "That's all I ask of you." He held out his hand.

That reminded Philip of the night they'd danced together a few days earlier. He took it.

Abel linked their fingers together and gently pulled Philip toward the kitchen.

Philip wasn't worried about Myron—he knew his son was in good hands with the other carriers.

The meeting in the kitchen was intimidating. All the people there were either alphas or council members, and Philip was just himself—a carrier, a man who'd been abused, a father to a newborn, a lost man who didn't have a home other than the one that had welcomed him when he'd been freed.

He held his chin high and stepped forward.

He could do this. The people in the room needed him, and he wasn't going to let them down, not when he was free thanks to them. "I want to help," he said.

Thomas smiled at him. "Thank you, Philip. Did Abel tell you what we'd like to hear from you?"

"Yes. I don't know how much I can tell you, but I'll do my best."

He let Abel steer him toward the only empty chair, probably Abel's before he'd gotten up. Philip sat in it and was relieved when Abel stayed behind him, a wall of strength and warmth at his back, reassuring.

He swallowed. "I can only think of one person who would be a good council member. Most of the people in the prickle bow down to Alpha Grimes. He's a cruel man, and he's used to getting what he wants. Everyone knows how bad things can go if they deny him, so they don't."

"Except for this one person."

"Yes. Oscar . . ." Philip hated saying that name out loud. "He told me she looked for me after he locked me in the room where Alex found me. She asked about me, tried to push Alpha Grimes to tell her what had happened to me. I don't know if he punished her for that or if he just ignored it. I was locked away by then. But she was always a nice person. She takes care of the kids when they fall and hurt themselves, or when Alpha Grimes or one of his goons get too rough. She's not an official healer, but she takes care of people."

"Who is she?"

"Karen. I—she's the only one I can think of that you'd want in the council. She'd do her best to keep everyone safe, and she's fair. She'd be a good alpha, too." No doubt better than Alpha Grimes had ever been. "But Alpha Grimes will never choose her as the prickle's council member. You have to know that."

Thomas nodded. "We do, but it's a start. Now we know we have an ally in the prickle. We might try to contact Karen and talk to her."

"That's good, but unless you find a way around Alpha Grimes, he's going to be the one who will choose the next council member, and he's going to choose someone like him, someone who will give him what he wants."

"This is only the first step, Philip. We can keep you updated if you want us to. We haven't decided how to deal with Grimes, but we'll find a way. We have to. No one here wants to spend the next twenty years having to hide you and the other carriers. We might not be like you, but you're our friends, our sons, our loved ones. You deserve to be free just as much as we are."

Philip was touched. He'd known Thomas cared—he had two carrier sons, and he'd done all he could to help them have the life they wanted. No one had ever cared for *Philip* that way, though. He could tell he was included in Thomas' words, and his chest felt warm and fuzzy. He'd never been part of a family, and now he was. It wasn't the family he'd dreamed of as a kid, a family where he'd have a husband and children, but he was still loved and protected, and so was Myron. No one cared who Myron's other father was. They loved him, and if something happened to Philip, they'd make sure Myron was okay.

The meeting broke up soon after that. Philip was relieved, because he hadn't felt he belonged, but he hoped he'd helped, even if only a bit. "Are you leaving right away?" he asked Abel, who hadn't left his side since he'd asked him to help.

"Well, there's nothing waiting for me at home. I live alone, you know, and I'm not a great cook, so if you and the others don't mind, I'd like to stay for pizza. I'll leave right after so I don't make you or anyone else uncomfortable."

"I don't think you make anyone here uncomfortable."

Abel cocked his head. "Not even you?"

He *did* make Philip feel awkward sometimes, but that was more because of how Philip felt around him than because of anything he did. "Not even me. I know you'd never hurt me or Myron. But sometimes I fall back into the past. When I do, it's too easy to imagine that everyone around here, and not just you, might hurt me."

"It's going to take you some time to heal."

"I know." But being free had helped enormously, as was having Myron with him. Philip knew Oscar would have taken his son away if he'd still been in the man's hands when he'd been born. Instead, Myron had been born free.

Some of the carriers had left the living room, but Chris and Jacob were still there. They were acting as if they were trying not to look at each other, and as soon as Chris saw Philip, he jumped to his feet. "Thank God you're here. I need to go to the bathroom." He thrust Myron into Abel's hands and rushed out, leaving both Abel and Philip blinking after him.

Philip reached for Myron, but Abel didn't move to give him to him. "Do you mind if I cuddle him a little? I've always loved babies. I used to hold Camden for hours when he was a baby."

"Of course not. It'll give my arms a break." Philip couldn't look away, not because he thought Abel might do something wrong, but because Abel looked good with Myron in his arms. "You're good with him."

Abel smiled down at Myron. "I like him. Sometimes I wish I had children."

"Why don't you?"

"Because I haven't found the right person to have them with. I'll admit I haven't looked very hard. My job takes a lot of my time. But maybe it's time to change that. I'm getting older, and I want to have a family."

Fear gripped Philip's stomach. Abel wanted a family, and that meant he'd have to find someone to share his life with. Philip desperately wanted to be that someone, but he couldn't say the words. He couldn't face rejection, and he was almost a hundred percent sure that was what would happen if he did tell Abel he wanted to be in his life.

And that *almost* was enough to keep him quiet.

CHAPTER THREE

The meeting with the other council members hadn't yield-
ed anything new. Abel wasn't surprised, but he wished
he hadn't had to listen to the raging of some of Oscar's
friends. They hadn't had a problem blaming just about anyone they didn't like, including Thomas and Morris, the two
alphas who'd had gone against them several times in the re-
cent past. Abel had almost laughed in their faces, but he'd
managed to stay quiet. He was always the quiet one, so no
one had been surprised.

The brakes on Oscar's car had been tampered with,
though. That was one thing the council was sure of now. Oscar was known to treat the road rules as optional, so he was
no doubt going too fast, and tampering with his brakes had
been enough to wrap him and his car around a tree, killing
him. The police were still working on the car, and maybe
they'd manage to find fingerprints or something, but Abel
doubted it. He didn't think they'd ever find out who was
behind the tampering, and that was okay with him. He
might not like the thought of a killer being loose in the forest, but he couldn't deny the man—or woman—had made
things easier for him and his friends, at least in part.

Of course, things would be even easier if Alpha Grimes
could be convinced to select a decent council member to take
Oscar's place. That was the reason Abel had come to the
prickle and was now asking the guard for entrance in porcupine territory. It was probably a stupid idea, and Grimes
had no reason to see Abel, but it was worth a try, or at least

Abel thought so.

"He says you can go in," the guard said. "Straight ahead. Alpha Grimes' house is the first one you'll see. Park in front of it and wait for someone to come get you."

"Thank you."

The guard grunted and opened the gate. Abel had never been in porcupine territory, but he suspected these were new security measures brought on by Oscar's death. It was surprising that he'd been allowed in, but he wasn't going to ask why. Maybe being the gentle and soft council member had helped. He knew he had a reputation, and while it might not be entirely true, he was willing to use it to get what he wanted.

He parked in front of the first house he saw. It was more like a big log cabin, and it was pretty in a way he hadn't expected. The council didn't have a lot of info on Grimes, so Abel wasn't sure if the alpha was married or if he had children. The fact that he'd wanted to use Vincent to carry a child indicated he might need an heir. The thought made Abel want to pound the asshole into the ground, but that wasn't why he was there, unfortunately.

The door opened just as he was closing the car door. He looked up, not surprised to see Alpha Grimes scowling at him from the porch. He inclined his head, knowing Grimes didn't want him to be there. The only reason he'd probably allowed it was that Abel was a council member, and he could create some problems for Grimes, even with some members of the council on Grimes' side.

"Council Member," Grimes said. He made it sound like it was torture for him to say those words.

Abel beamed at him. "Alpha Grimes. Thank you for agreeing to see me."

"I didn't have much of a choice. What do you want?"

So this is how they were going to play it? Abel wasn't

surprised. "To talk to you."

Grimes crossed his arms over his chest. "About what? The fact that you and your people killed Oscar?"

Again, Abel wasn't surprised. "Are you saying *I* had something to do with it?"

. "Of course not," he backpedaled. "But I do think someone in the council ordered Oscar's death. You needed him out to get one of your people in his place. That's not gonna happen."

"You can, of course, bring every concern you have to the council. We're already investigating Oscar's death. He might not have been a friend of mine, but that doesn't mean I and others don't want to find out who killed him. The council was created to keep peace and justice in the forest, and that's what we're going to do."

Grimes snorted. Abel expected him to tell him to fuck off, but instead, he asked, "What do you want, then?"

Abel decided that going straight to the point was probably the best thing he could do in this situation. "I'd like to know if you already have an idea of who you're going to nominate as the next council member for the porcupines."

"You want to be the one to pick."

"That's not what I said." It was what Abel wanted, but he knew better than to say it. Grimes would use whatever he could against Abel and his side of the council.

"I'm not going to choose one of your minions."

"I don't know anyone in your prickle, so that would be hard. But I'd like to remind you that it's a known fact that the two deer carriers who were taken from my herd ended up here, and that you were planning to rape one of them." Officially, Camden and Vincent were still with the council. Everyone knew they weren't, though, including obviously Grimes.

Grimes' face reddened. "You have no proof."

Abel had Vincent's word, but both he and Grimes knew he couldn't use that, not when Vincent was supposed to be in council custody and was hiding out in cete territory instead. "Maybe not. But the council isn't blind to what's happening here and in other territories. There is no majority right now, but that doesn't mean we can't do anything."

"Who? What's your pick?"

"Karen." Abel didn't know the woman, but he trusted Philip.

Grimes shook his head. "I'm not going to choose that know-it-all bitch. Forget it. And forget that the prickle is going to help you in any way. *I'll* be the one choosing the next council member, and I'll do it keeping the prickle's best interest in mind."

More than the prickle's interest, Grimes was going to keep *his* in mind when he chose. Abel knew it, and he was sure Grimes was aware of that.

There was nothing Abel could do, though. Short of killing Grimes, it seemed like the man was going to choose another asshole of Oscar's caliber. That meant the council would be back to having a majority of people who sought power and money more than the good of the people they were supposed to protect, and Abel couldn't allow that.

He didn't know how to stop it, though.

He wasn't a killer. He didn't even watch horror movies, because there was always too much blood and gore. And as a council member, he couldn't order or pay someone to kill Grimes. He might be ready to do just about anything to keep Philip and everyone else safe, but he drew the line at murder.

He hoped he was one of the few, though.

He didn't know everything Grimes and Oscar had done, but what he *did* know was enough to convince him that Grimes deserved to die just as much as Oscar. He'd been complicit in what had been done to Philip and what had almost happened to Camden and Vincent. Abel wouldn't be surprised if Grimes had his hands in some kind of carrier trafficking. He had no way to prove it, but he wouldn't have to if Grimes ended up dead.

That was the only solution Abel could think of, but he didn't know what to do about it. He straightened his back and looked Grimes in the eyes. "You're going to regret it if you go against the council. Oscar might have shielded you and your traffic until now, but the prickle is exposed. No matter how fast you choose someone else, it's going to take them a while to have the kind of power needed to cover what's happening here, whatever that is." Things couldn't be worse than they already were. With Oscar dead, the council was at a standstill, and Abel knew he and his friends needed to tilt that somehow. Talking to Grimes had been a last-resort attempt, and with these results, they were going to have to find a way around him.

Or over his dead body.

Philip's thoughts were never far from Oscar since he'd found out his captor was dead. He wasn't sorry for what had happened to him, but he couldn't help but wonder who had killed him. Was it another council member who needed him out of the way? One of the men Philip saw regularly? He wouldn't have blamed them if they'd been behind this, but he wasn't sure he could look at them the same way if that was what had happened.

He realized he was too soft. He wanted his son to grow up safe, even if he ended up being a carrier, and that would only happen if the council members were humane. Oscar hadn't been. He'd been a monster, and the world was a better place without him in it. Philip was still uneasy, though.

And what if it wasn't a council member? Most of them were good people, and Philip had a hard time believing one of them could do this. Maybe it was naïve of him, though. He knew they were all ready to do anything to make sure their people were safe, and that included Philip and the other carriers now.

And if it wasn't one of the council members, *who* had done it? An alpha? Maybe Alpha Grimes instead, after Oscar had lost Philip, Camden, and Vincent? Philip wouldn't have been surprised to find out that was what had happened, but he had his doubts. No matter what Oscar had done, he'd been useful to Alpha Grimes, and that hadn't ended when Philip and the others had been rescued.

Maybe it had been a porcupine shifter. They all hated Oscar and Alpha Grimes, except of course the people who got something out of what they were doing. Alpha Grimes had surrounded himself with guards he knew were on his side, and his beta was as much of an asshole as he was, but maybe someone else in the prickle had managed to find their spine. It wouldn't have been hard for one of them to get to Oscar's car while it was parked in front of his house. It would have been easy, actually.

Myron's gurgles tore Philip from his thoughts. He was grateful for the interruption. He didn't *want* to think about Oscar and Alpha Grimes. If he had things his way, he'd never give them a second thought.

It was wishful thinking, though. No matter how much Philip hated the two men, he couldn't deny Oscar was Myron's father, at least in the biological sense. That left him with questions about what he was going to tell Myron.

"What's wrong?" Kaspar asked. He'd been reading in the corner while Philip played with Myron on the couch. He was so quiet Philip had forgotten he was there.

"Nothing."

Kaspar closed his book. He left his thumb in it to find his page, but he shifted his focus to Philip. "Are you sure? You've been quiet the past few days. Well, you've always been quiet, but it's been worse lately."

Kaspar was one of the oldest carriers in the house, right after Philip. He was twenty-five while most of the other carriers were in their early twenties, if even that. Vincent, as well as Chris and Nico, were only nineteen, while Camden was the youngest at seventeen. That thought made Philip's stomach churn, because he knew what Oscar had been planning to do to Camden.

It was a good thing he was dead, no matter how that had happened.

Not only was Kaspar one of the oldest, he was one of the quietest. He loved to read, and Philip knew he worried about the other people who lived in the house and the people he'd left behind when he'd had to leave the sleuth. At least he got to see a lot of bear shifters he'd probably grown up with, since half of the house's security was taken care of by the sleuth. He cared about everyone, though, as his obvious worry over what Philip had been thinking showed.

Philip sighed. He knew keeping everything to himself wasn't good. He was so used to it that it was second nature for him, though. "I was thinking about Oscar."

Chris would have berated Philip for giving the dead man even one second of his thoughts, but Kaspar didn't. Instead, he grabbed a piece of paper from the coffee table and stuck it into his book. "Do you want to talk about it?" he then asked.

"I don't know. I know I shouldn't think about Oscar anymore because he's dead and he was a cruel bastard, but he's never going to be completely gone from my life, not when he was Myron's father."

"But he wasn't, not really. I mean, he helped you create Myron, but *you're* Myron's father. He was just a sperm donor."

"I know. But what do I tell Myron when he grows up and asks about his father?"

Kaspar smiled. "Well, I hope by then you and Abel will have pulled your heads out of your asses and will be married and Myron will have two fathers. If that hasn't happened and you *do* want to tell him about Oscar, though, I'd suggest starting by telling him that his sperm donor was a bad man who hurt you, but that you got *him* out of it and that you're happy. I think the trick here will be being honest about Oscar and what he did while making sure Myron understands that he's not like Oscar and that you love him."

Philip ignored the way Kaspar's words made his heart flutter. He could too easily imagine how life would be if he and Abel got married, and Abel would be such a good father for Myron. That wasn't what he was supposed to think about, though. "I think he should know who his biological father was. I hate the thought of ever telling him about it, but he has a right to know, and it will be better for him to hear it from me than from gossip or people who want to hurt him."

Kaspar leaned over and patted Philip's knee. "You have time to think about that, Philip. Even if you do want to have that conversation with Myron, it's not going to happen for more than a decade. Don't obsess over it already. It's no use. You should focus on your life and on making yourself and your son happy." He grinned. "And Abel, possibly."

Philip's cheeks heated. "Can we not talk about him?"

"Of course, if that's what you want. I know Chris never shuts up about it and that he can be a bit much sometimes. But, and this is the last thing I'll say about it, I think you should give yourself a chance. You and Abel would be good together."

Philip was relieved when Kaspar grabbed his book and

left the living room. What he'd said made sense, except for the last bit. That wasn't something Philip wanted to think about.

He wiggled his fingers in front of Myron's face, smiling when Myron caught one of them. It was almost time for Myron's nap, and Philip was going to try to sleep, too. Myron had been agitated the past few nights, and Philip hadn't been sleeping well, not even between feedings.

The front door opened. Philip leaned back against the couch to peek at the entrance, hoping it wasn't Chris. He loved the guy, but he'd been obsessed with getting Philip to admit he was in love with Abel, and that wasn't something Philip would ever say out loud.

It was Joel, though, and Philip relaxed. "Are you here for lunch?" he asked when Joel walked into the living room. "Because you missed it. I'm sure we can come up with something for you, though."

"Nope, not here for lunch. I ate with Eddie. But Arlene will be coming around in an hour or so, and she wanted me to tell you she wants to check in on you."

Arlene was the cete's healer, and she'd helped Philip deliver Myron. She regularly checked in on him and examined him to make sure he was healthy. He'd been malnourished when he'd arrived, and while Oscar hadn't beaten him after he'd found out Philip was expecting a boy, that didn't mean he hadn't done so in the past. Some of Philip's old broken bones still ached some days.

"I can't say I'm looking forward to her poking and prodding me, but I'll see her."

Joel grinned. "It's not like you have a choice."

Philip did. No one would force him to submit to a medical examination, or anything else. But he owed it to himself and to Myron to be as healthy as he could, and that meant letting Arlene poke him to her heart's content, unfortunately.

Abel waved at Arlene, the cete's healer, as he got out of his car. She was taking out a bag from her trunk, and he rushed to her side to help her. "I'll carry this inside."

She smiled at him. "Thank you. What are you doing here, Council Member Porter?"

Abel grimaced. "Please, call me Abel. I feel we've seen each other often enough in the past few months."

"That we have."

Arlene was in charge of keeping the carriers and the guards who lived at the Bishop house healthy. She visited every month or so to talk to them and examine the ones she thought needed more help. "Who are you visiting today?"

"I suppose I might as well tell you. I'm here for Philip, although of course, I'll see anyone who needs me to."

"Is he okay?" Abel hadn't heard anything about Philip being ill, but people weren't going to call him specifically to tell him that. He and Philip were friends, but that was it, no matter how much Abel wanted more.

"It's just a routine check. I'll check Myron, too."

Abel relaxed. It was only three months since Philip had given birth, so it made sense that both he and Myron needed to see Arlene more often than the others.

Abel carried Arlene's bag to the back room she used for her examinations, then he went back to the front of the house. Philip was already there, Myron in his arms as he spoke with Arlene. He smiled at Abel, and when he and Arlene disappeared into the back room with Myron, Abel couldn't help but hang around and wait. He knew he should go to the living room or the kitchen and find something to do. He wasn't even sure why he'd decided to come to the house.

That wasn't true. He'd come because he wanted to see Philip, but he couldn't tell Philip that. What would he think? Hopefully, no one would ask him what he was doing there, because he didn't want to lie.

The door opened after about fifteen minutes, and Philip walked out. He was holding Myron and looked around. "Why is everyone gone when I need them?" he grumbled.

Abel stepped forward. "What do you need?"

"I have to give Myron to one of them so that Arlene can check me. Have you seen anyone? Kaspar was in the living room earlier."

"No, but you can give Myron to me. That is, if you trust me with him, of course." Abel didn't want to assume anything, even though he'd held Myron more than once since he was born. That didn't mean Philip trusted him, but Abel liked to think he did.

Philip hesitated. "Are you sure? Aren't you here for a meeting or something?"

Abel was not going to blush. He couldn't. "Actually, no. I, well, I wanted to see you. Find out how you were doing."

Philip's eyes widened. "Really?"

"Yes. So why don't you give me Myron and get back to Arlene? We'll be here when you're done, in the living room. I promise I'll take good care of him."

Philip smiled. "I know you will."

Abel stretched his arms and gently took Myron. He knew Philip trusted him, but it always touched him when it happened. After what Philip had gone through, being trusted by him was something that made Abel feel proud. "He ate earlier, and it's time for his nap, but with the visit, I don't think he'll go down easily. Call me if you need help, okay?" Philip said.

"I won't need help, but I promise to let you know if anything happens. Go on. Arlene is waiting for you."

47

"Are you sure you want to do this? I can find someone else. You're not used to spending time with babies, and Myron can be—"

"Go, Philip. I'm looking forward to spending some time with Myron." Usually, Abel didn't get enough of it. He was going to enjoy this.

Philip finally went back to the room, and Abel took Myron to the living room. He sat into one of the armchairs and settled Myron in his lap, gently cooing at him. He felt like an idiot, but Myron's gummy smiles were worth it.

Abel could see Myron was tired, though, so he held him close and hummed. He didn't have a song in mind, but the sound and the vibrations seemed to relax Myron, which was what Abel had been going for. He stroked Myron's warm, soft skin, the wispy hair tickling his fingertips. He could feel Myron slipping into sleep, his breath puffing against Abel's cheek.

Abel continued to hum. He was tired, and he closed his eyes. He could rest for a bit until Philip got back. Then they could maybe spend the afternoon together. Abel wanted to forget what had happened earlier with Grimes. He felt dirty for having threatened the man, even though he knew Grimes deserved it, and anything else that came his way.

That wasn't Abel, though. Maybe he was too soft to be a council member, but he didn't want anyone to be hurt, and he certainly didn't want to threaten people. That wasn't why he'd accepted the council member job. No, he'd accepted it because he wanted to do good, to help people. Myron's slight weight reminded him that he *had* helped and that he could continue to. Myron and Philip would have still been in Oscar's hands if Abel and the others on the right side hadn't intervened.

Maybe Abel should push his softness aside until the people he'd sworn to protect were safe and could live their life the way they intended.

"So everything is fine?" Philip asked as he put his clothes back on. He hated these visits, but he trusted Arlene. She wouldn't take advantage of his nudity.

He'd been wary of her in the beginning, just like he'd been wary of pretty much everyone but Abel, but he'd gotten over that quickly. He'd been seven months pregnant when he'd been rescued, and that had meant that Arlene had examined him and taken blood too many times for him to keep count. Then there had been the birth, and that was when all of Philip's fears about what she might do flew out the window. He hadn't been able to focus on anything but the pain, and she'd been right there with him, helping him through it and making sure he and his baby made it.

Arlene looked up from her notebook. "Yep, everything is fine. You've healed perfectly, your blood pressure is good, and since you haven't reported anything, I'd say you're good to go." She grinned. "And I'm giving you the okay to be intimate again."

Philip blinked. "What?"

"You know. To have sex. As I said, you're healed, so that won't be a problem."

Philip's cheeks flushed. "I don't—who would I have sex with? Wait, don't answer that. I don't want to know." He was pretty sure he knew what Arlene was thinking anyway, and he didn't want to hear it. He already got enough of that from everyone in the Bishop house.

Arlene chuckled. "All right. I'm just saying that if that's what was stopping you, you can forget about it."

Philip shook his head. "That's not—you know what? This isn't your business."

"You're right, it isn't, and I don't expect you to tell me

anything you don't want to share." She sobered up. "But I wish I could do more. I realize that your body is probably not the only thing stopping you from getting close to Abel. I know what you've been through, and I know it's hard to get over something like that. You know you can call me if you need anything, even if it's only an ear to listen to you. I won't judge."

Philip was even more uncomfortable now. "I know." He finished dressing and shuffled toward the door. "Can I go?"

"Of course. I'll see you in a few months, unless you need anything before that. Like birth control, maybe? Just give me a call."

Philip almost ran out of the room. He knew Arlene's concern came from a good place, but he wasn't going to need birth control. He wasn't even sure he'd manage to let anyone touch him, let alone have sex. He dreamed about it sometimes, and Abel starred in every single one of those dreams. But when it came to it, even if he did have the possibility of doing it, he had no way of knowing if he'd actually be able to. Oscar had been the only one Philip had been with that way, and he'd hated that. So far, sex had only been pain and humiliation for him. Could he get over it?

He shook his head. It was a moot point, wasn't it? Abel had never done or said anything that would make him think he wanted him that way.

"Abel?" he called out. Abel had said he and Myron would be in the living room, so Philip went there. He stopped at the door and leaned against the doorframe, smiling at the sight in front of him.

Abel was sitting in one of the armchairs, Myron in his arms. They were both asleep, from what Philip could see from where he was.

It was adorable.

Abel always looked gentle. Philip had never heard him

yell or seen him angry, even when it had been warranted. Philip wasn't sure whether it was because Abel just was that way, or if he was careful when Philip was around, but it didn't matter. Abel was always gentle, and he looked even softer in his sleep.

His expression was slack, and he was holding onto Myron in a way that made Philip sure he wouldn't drop him, not even in his sleep.

God, he yearned for this. He wanted a life where finding Abel and Myron asleep on the couch was familiar, where he didn't have to expect a moment when Abel would leave. He wanted a family, a man who would love him even after what had been done to him, a man who wouldn't think he was fragile or tainted.

Could he ever have that? He didn't know, but Abel made him want to hope.

Philip swallowed. Since they were both asleep, he could go to the kitchen to prepare a snack. They'd both be hungry when they woke up, and to be honest, he enjoyed the time alone. It forced him to think of things he usually did his best to ignore, but it was nice not to feel needed, not to have to worry about anyone else but himself for a few hours.

He was relieved that the kitchen was empty, for once. He made himself a sandwich, ate it, then got a second one ready for Abel.

The back door opened, startling him. He was so used to hiding in this kind of situation that he didn't even think about it before slipping into the pantry. His heart was racing, and it took him a second to calm down enough to realize what was happening.

It was Chris and Jacob. They wouldn't hurt him. He was safe.

"Chris, we shouldn't do this," Jacob said, his voice barely louder than a whisper. Philip wouldn't have heard him if he hadn't been hiding in the pantry, and he felt awkward at being there listening in. He didn't want to. He hadn't *meant* to, but now he was stuck. He wasn't sure which would be worse — to stay there and listen to the rest of a private conversation, or to come out and have to explain what he was doing in there.

Chris and Jacob would probably understand, but Philip wasn't sure he could stand the pity in their gaze,

"We're not doing anything," Chris answered. He was louder, as if he didn't care who heard him.

"You know what I mean."

"Yeah, I do, and I don't understand why you can't be with me. You like me, don't you? We work well together. We fit."

"And I don't understand how you think it can work. I'm just a guard. You're a future alpha. Your father won't accept this. Not a lot of people would."

"Who cares? I'll kick their asses when I'm the alpha."

"Chris —"

"No. I thought you liked me. I'm not asking you to marry me, for fuck's sake. I just want to see where this can go. I want to be *happy*. My father isolated Nico and me because he was afraid someone would find out what we are. This is the first time I'm free to choose someone and to be with him, and I want *you*. Doesn't that matter?"

"It does, but, Chris —"

"Right. Of course what other people think is more important. I guess you don't care for me *that* much. I shouldn't be surprised. Everyone always wants me because I'm going to be the alpha, but tell them I'm a carrier and they either try to fuck me or run the other way."

Philip heard footsteps stomping out of the kitchen. He held his breath, wondering if Chris had been the only one who'd left or if Jacob had gone with him. He couldn't exactly stay in the pantry forever.

"You can come out," Jacob said.

Philip's eyes widened. How had he known? What was Philip supposed to do?

He walked out. "I'm sorry. I didn't mean to listen to your conversation. The door slammed open, and I freaked out. Bad memories," he said without looking at Jacob.

Jacob sighed. "It's okay. I guess you haven't learned anything new anyway, huh? Everyone around here knows Chris is interested in me."

Philip cleared his throat. "And you're interested in him, aren't you?"

"I am."

"But you don't think you should be together." Philip could understand that. He had the same reservations, the same obstacles stopping him from even telling Abel he was in love with him. Abel was a council member, so why should he want Philip? And even if he did, it couldn't work because no one would be okay with it.

It wasn't fair. It was obvious even to Philip that Chris and Jacob cared for each other. Why should they stay away just because a small group of people had decided that carriers couldn't be alphas and that they should be the ones deciding who married who? Why should anyone else decide Philip's future or Chris'? They were the ones in charge of their lives. They should make their own decisions about it.

CHAPTER FOUR

A bel hated answering the phone. It was never good news, not lately. Maybe he could give Philip a phone and the instructions to call him whenever he wanted. At least that would give him something good to look forward to.

Abel sighed as he took his cell from the desk. At least it was Morris. Abel liked Morris. "Hello?"

"Am I disturbing you?"

"No. What happened now?"

Morris chuckled. "I could be calling you to chat."

"I don't think so. We both have too much to do to chat in the middle of the day." Although Abel would make an exception for Philip.

"You're right, we do. We got an anonymous tip that the minks and the opossums have carriers."

Abel swore. "How did we not know about this before? Wait, never mind. I already know the answer to that." The minks and the opossums weren't on the *right side,* as Abel had started thinking of himself and the others who were trying to get the rest of the council to do the right thing. They hadn't had much luck until now, and Grimes still hadn't chosen a new council member for the prickle. Not that choosing someone would have changed things. He'd been clear enough about that when Abel had talked to him.

"Thomas is calling a meeting."

Abel's stomach flip-flopped. "Where and when?"

"Bishop house, in a few hours."

That was good. "Why the Bishop house? Isn't it dangerous? Won't it bring attention to the house?"

"We trust everyone who's invited to the meeting, and it gives them and us the opportunity to spend some time with the family members they have there. I'm sure Alpha Wiley will be happy to see Chris and Nico. It's been a while since he managed to come. And *you* can have a chat with Philip. A little birdie told me you fell asleep with Myron the other day and that the two of you looked precious."

"Tell that little birdie that if I get my hands on him, I'll strangle him."

Morris laughed. "I doubt you will. See you in a few hours?"

"Of course." As if Abel would miss the meeting. Even if he hadn't wanted to see Philip, he needed to keep up with what was happening, and he didn't have anything better to do. The council was almost at a standstill, since they were missing one member and they couldn't make major decisions if they weren't complete. The only thing they did when they met was yell at each other and fight, and that was something Abel *definitely* could do without.

Since Abel didn't have anything better to do, he left his house as soon as he and Morris hung up. He felt giddy, and he knew exactly why. He'd already told himself too many times to count that he shouldn't feel that way, but he felt like he and Philip were growing closer. It was probably just an impression—Philip was kind to everyone, and of course he'd say yes when Abel tried to help him with Myron. He was a single dad to a newborn. He needed some rest and sleep, and it was easier to get that when someone helped him with the baby. But Abel's heart couldn't help but hope, and Abel hoped it wasn't going to end up broken. Philip would let him down nicely if he ever found out about the enormous crush Abel had on him, but that didn't mean it wouldn't hurt.

Morris and Thomas were already there when Abel arrived at the Bishop house. Dan was there, too, talking with his sons in a corner of the living room. "Are we doing this here this time?" Abel asked as he sat next to Morris on the couch. He looked around, hoping to see Philip, but he wasn't there.

Of course, It caught Morris' attention, and he grinned at Abel. "We thought we would, since there are more of us coming. And he's upstairs."

Abel didn't bother behaving like he didn't know who Morris was talking about. "I'll go find him when the meeting is over."

The conversation between Dan and one of the twins—Abel suspected it was Chris because of the way he was answering his father—wasn't going well. Chris got up and stomped away, ignoring his father's call for him to come back. Abel winced. Was this what Philip could look forward to with Myron? The baby was still a newborn, but he'd grow up to become a nineteen-year-old, and Abel wasn't sure he was looking forward to that. Of course, he might not be in Myron's life by the time he reached that age. He hoped he would, though.

Nico patted his father's shoulder and went after his brother. Dan raked a hand through his hair and flopped back into the armchair he was sitting in. "How did you do this, Thomas? You have three sons. How did you deal with them wanting to be with people who aren't suitable for them?"

Thomas arched a brow. "I supposed you're asking about Joel and Eddie?"

Dan shrugged. "I don't know what I'm asking. Chris is next in line to take my place, and the person who will be by his side has to be able to deal with that."

"Jacob is a good man. Chris could do worse."

"Does everyone know about this?"

"I'm pretty sure you were the last one to find out. I'm not saying they're going to get married, but you should let Chris make this kind of decision for himself. That's what we're fighting for. Besides, he's only nineteen. He and Jacob might not be together when this mess is over and Chris and Nico can go home."

Dan rubbed his forehead. "Chris is a carrier, though."

"He is, but you have daughters. Did you freak out this much when they started dating?"

Dan scowled. "Of course I did."

Morris chuckled. "There's plenty of condoms around the house, so I don't think you have to worry about that. Besides, from what I know of Chris, he has his head on his shoulders, and he knows what he wants. He'll be a good alpha one day, but not if you tape his wings down now."

Abel was so glad he didn't have kids right now. He was younger than the other three men, though, so maybe by the time he was their age, he would. He couldn't help but think of Myron when he thought of that future. This was what he wanted — to worry about Myron, to make sure he grew up having all the possibilities life could offer him.

A few other people filtered in, and by the time the meeting started, there were close to fifteen people crammed into the living room. Abel was glad he'd arrived early.

"How did you find out about these carriers?" Jerome asked. The fox alpha looked tired, but then Abel supposed they all did.

"It was an anonymous letter," Morris told him. "I found it on my porch this morning, and before you ask, no, I have no idea how whoever wrote it managed to sneak past our security. It didn't smell like bear, though, so I doubt it's one of my sleuth members. I'm looking into it, but from what I know, I doubt whoever is behind this wants to hurt the sleuth or our alliance. It looks more like they want to save the carriers we didn't know about."

"What do we do?"

"We need to check in on them," Dan said. He was always protective of the carriers, probably because of his sons.

"How? I doubt the mink and opossum alphas are going to let us waltz into their territory to see them."

"What about Alex and his friends?" Abel asked. "They went into porcupine territory and saved Philip, Vincent, and Camden. They also got Josiah out of his father's hands."

"We could build a team," Morris agreed. "One member for each of us, so we're all participating."

Abel liked that idea, but no matter how much he thought about it, he couldn't come up with anyone from the herd who could fit into that kind of team. He continued thinking as they filed out of the room once the meeting was over. Almost all the alphas and council members had someone in mind, but not him.

"You're thinking hard," Thomas said.

Abel shrugged. "I don't think I can offer you a deer shifter for your team. You know us—we're gentle and soft. No one in the herd has that kind of training, not even the guards." Abel chuckled. "Look at me. We're pretty much all built the same way, and I doubt you want a chubby, clumsy deer shifter to mess things up on this kind of mission."

"You're not clumsy," someone snapped.

Abel blinked. He didn't think he'd ever seen Philip angry, yet there he was, standing in front of him and glaring at him.

Philip didn't like hearing Abel talk about himself that way. He wasn't sure why he'd said it out loud, though. He couldn't take the words back, and he didn't want to, but he wished he didn't feel like everyone was staring at him.

"I'll leave the two of you to it," Thomas said. "But Abel, don't worry about this. Not everyone is fit for this kind of team, and that's okay. You and Rod are already helping enough as it is. We can take care of the team, and of course, we'll keep the two of you updated with the progress and anything they might find once they go."

Abel nodded. "Thank you. I'll talk to Rod, just in case he thinks of someone, but I wouldn't hold my breath if I were you."

"What's going on?" Philip asked when Thomas left. "Why were you talking badly of yourself?"

Abel smiled. "I wasn't. I was just explaining to Thomas that I might not be able to find a deer shifter for the team we're putting together." Abel sighed. "We got news that the minks and the opossums have carriers in their territory. We're going to try to get to them, at the very least to make sure they're okay and treated decently, but the minks and the opossums aren't going to let us into their territory. Their council members voted for the carrier law, so it's a fair guess to think they're doing whatever they want with the poor guys."

"So you're sending a team?"

"Yes. I don't know if Alex is going to continue being part of it now that he's married and Seamus is expecting, but it's going to be like the small team that freed you, Camden, and Vincent."

Philip didn't like to think about that night, but he was relieved that if carriers were being abused, they were going to be helped. "I'm sorry."

Abel blinked. "What for?"

"For barging in into your conversation. I just came downstairs to get Myron a bottle. He's going to wake up soon."

"You didn't barge into our conversation."

Philip snorted.

Abel chuckled. "All right, maybe you did," he admitted. "And I'm still not sure what that was about, so why don't you go get Myron's bottle ready and we can go upstairs to talk about it?"

Philip blushed. "What if I don't want to talk about it?" He didn't like hearing Abel berating himself, but he realized now that he'd been ridiculous. But he thought the world of Abel, and he couldn't understand how Abel didn't see that.

"We don't have to, but I'd like to hear what you meant when you said I wasn't clumsy."

"Well, you're not."

"A bit."

Philip sighed. He was going to have to do this, wasn't he? "I just . . . it sounded like you were serious when you were saying you're, well, chubby and clumsy, and I don't like that you think that of yourself."

Abel arched a brow. "Then the same goes for yourself."

"What are you talking about?"

"Go get Myron's bottle. We'll talk upstairs."

Philip wanted to push, but he could tell he wasn't going to get anything else from Abel until they were alone. It wasn't a bad thing—he could do without everyone else in the house hearing their conversation. There were too many curious ears, especially Chris'. He always wanted to know everything, and he tried to fix it—as if he could. That was probably the future alpha in him.

Abel was waiting at the bottom of the stairs when Philip got back with the bottle. They didn't talk as they climbed up, and Philip felt like his skin was crawling. He hated the anticipation. He wasn't even sure what they were supposed to talk about.

"You don't like it when I think and talk badly of myself," Abel said once they were in the bedroom that Philip shared with Myron. Myron was still asleep, and Abel was whispering, but Philip heard him.

He peeked into the crib. "You're right, I don't."

"Why not?"

"Because you're not—"

"I wasn't lying when I said I was clumsy and chubby. It was just an observation. I'm not blind, and I can see I'm not as well-built as, let's say, the guards around here."

"That doesn't mean it's a bad thing." Philip liked that Abel was softer. It made him feel warm and welcome.

"I never said it was. Just like what you went through doesn't make you less."

Philip didn't want to talk about this, but he was the one who'd brought it up. He put the bottle next to the crib and sat on the bed. "I never said—"

"You didn't say it, but it doesn't take a genius to know that's what you're thinking. What happened to you is terrible, but it didn't change you, not the way you think. I didn't know you before, but you're a good man, and a great father. What you've been through will always leave its mark on you, but just like you don't like me thinking bad things about myself, I don't like you doing the same. Because when I look at you, I don't see a victim or whatever else you think I see. I see a gorgeous, brave man anyone would be lucky to have in their life."

"You really think that?" Philip hated how vulnerable he sounded, but he needed the reassurance, especially coming from Abel.

"Of course I do. And it doesn't have anything to do with you being a carrier. That's part of who you are, but it's not all of you."

Myron whimpered, and Philip moved toward him. Abel got there before he did, though, and Philip stayed back, watching him take Myron in his arms, cooing at him and trying to soothe him. Philip already knew Abel was good with

Myron, so he watched, not intervening.

Giving up control over his son was hard. He'd been My-ron's only caretaker since Myron was born. Even when he had things to do and he had to leave Myron to someone else, it was easy, because the carriers were his friends. Abel was Philip's friend, too, but there was so much more to it.

Philip could imagine this was his life—a life where he and Abel were together, and Abel routinely took care of Myron like he was now. He'd be a good father to Myron. He cared about people and always tried to do the right thing. And what he'd just told Philip made Philip hope.

Could he and Abel *actually* be together? Abel hadn't said he wanted Philip that way, but he'd made it sound like he did. Or was Philip imagining things? He wasn't sure of any-thing anymore. He wanted to believe, but he was afraid to get hurt. It would be so much easier to stay back and let things go the way they were going. It was comfortable. It was nice.

But was *nice* enough for Philip? Now that he knew he had the possibility of an new life in front of him, could he settle for watching the man he was falling in love with from afar? Could he stand being just friends with Abel when he might have a chance for more?

What would happen if Philip told Abel he loved him and Abel didn't feel the same way? It would hurt, that was for sure, but Philip knew Abel. Abel wouldn't be cruel about it. Things would be awkward between them for a while, but Abel wouldn't push Philip out of his life. They'd still be friends. The only thing Philip would lose was the hope that they could be more, so he wouldn't be worse off than he al-ready was.

Did he have the courage to step forward, though? Abel had said he thought Philip was brave, but Philip felt any-thing but.

Abel wanted to stay forever, but evening was falling, and Philip no doubt had things to do. Myron was asleep again after they'd played with him for part of the afternoon, and Abel needed to talk to Rod. Maybe his alpha could think of someone to put on the team. Abel knew he'd want to participate, but being deer shifters, they were starting with a disadvantage.

They weren't ferocious like bear shifters. They couldn't hide well like weasel shifters. They were deer. They took up space and ate grass. That was about all they could do.

"I'm going to go," he murmured.

Philip and Myron were on the bed, Myron on his back with Philip hunched over him, watching him like he was a miracle. And he was, just like all newborns were.

Philip looked up. "You can stay for dinner."

"I wish I could, but I need to talk to Rod, and my sister will want news from Camden." Abel hesitated. He always ended up at the Bishop house for meetings, but rarely for something nice. "I could come back tomorrow, or the day after that. Maybe we can have lunch together."

Philip's eyes widened just a bit, enough for Abel to know he was surprised. "You want to have lunch with me?"

"Of course I do." He wanted everything with Philip, but he knew how hesitant Philip was. Abel didn't know why that was, and he wasn't going to ask, but maybe he'd been taking things too slow with him. He didn't think Philip was aware of how much he wanted him in his life, and maybe that was a mistake. Philip couldn't make a decision if he didn't know there was one to make.

"You can come whenever you want. It's not like I have things to do."

Abel grimaced. "I'm sorry you can't leave the house."

"I'm not. I feel safe here." And he'd probably needed it. The men who should have kept him safe had brutalized him. It couldn't have been easy to trust again, especially people he didn't know.

Abel wanted to lean forward and kiss Philip's forehead, but instead, he smiled and left the bedroom, silently closing the door behind himself.

He managed to get to the front door without anyone seeing him. He didn't care if someone did, but he'd rather not answer questions about what he'd been doing in Philip's bedroom for most of the afternoon, and he knew Philip wouldn't want to, either. No one would disturb him, though, not with Myron sleeping. Abel, on the other hand, was fair game, and he was relieved when he snuck out of the door still on his own.

Of course, that didn't last long. He was sliding into his car when the front door opened and Eddie came out. He was alone, something that didn't happen often, and he waved at Abel.

Abel sighed and waited for Eddie to come to his door. "Hey, do you mind giving me a ride? I came with Joel, but he took the car back to his parents' house. Wanted to talk to his mom."

Since Abel had to pass by the alpha's house, he couldn't very well say no. Besides, he didn't want to. Eddie wasn't like Chris, who wouldn't have cared about privacy and would have asked all the questions he could think of. "Climb in."

"Thanks."

Abel bit his lower lip. Maybe meeting Eddie right now could help him. He, like everyone else in the forest, had grown up hearing that carriers were made for alphas, to carry their babies and give them heirs. That was why carriers were always matched with alphas, and the tradition had continued even after the council had been formed. Things were changing, though, and Eddie wasn't an alpha, even though he was married to a carrier.

Abel had always known that rule was stupid—carriers were people, and they should be able to choose who they wanted to marry, not be traded like livestock—but he wasn't quite sure how to deal with changing it himself.

He swallowed. He supposed he should ask and see what Eddie would tell him. "You and Joel . . ." he started, but he was unsure how to go on.

"You want to know how it is to be married to a carrier even though I'm not an alpha and I'll never be one."

Abel relaxed. "Yes. I'm not saying it's wrong, of course. The only important thing is that you're both happy. But how do you deal with everyone else? Have they been accepting?" The last thing Abel wanted was for Philip to have to face more abuse from intolerant people.

"It's a mixed bunch. The people around here don't care, of course, but some of the alphas and council members have said stuff, and of course, when we get into town, we have to listen to idiots who think Joel should have been married to an alpha. Neither of us would change what happened, though." He smiled. "Are you asking because of Philip?"

Abel groaned. "Does everyone know about it?"

"Pretty much."

"Chris has a big mouth."

"That he does, but it's not just him. Everyone with eyes has noticed the way the two of you look at each other. I'm pretty sure the guards have a bet going on as to who is going to break down and tell the other they're in love with him and how long it's going to take."

Abel grimaced. He hated when other people stuck their noses into his life, but he supposed it was okay in this case. Everyone at the Bishop house loved Philip, and they no doubt wanted him to be happy. Why they thought Abel could do that, Abel wasn't sure, but he was ready to try. He *wanted* to make Philip happy. "I do like him."

"Only like? That's fine, of course, but I think he's in love with you, and I'd hate to see him hurt. Not that you could do anything, but you know how it is."

"All right, all right. I'm in love with him. How could I not?"

"I don't know. Some people would be wary of his past."

"I don't care about his past. He had no choice in what was done to him, and I love that he survived it. How many people would be the way he is today after all that? If anything, I admire him and how strong he is."

"And Myron?"

Abel could tell Eddie was making sure he wouldn't hurt Philip. It was the kind of chat he might have had with Philip's father if the man had cared about his son, albeit in a roundabout way. Eddie cared for Philip. Everyone who knew him did, and it warmed Abel's heart. Philip would never be alone anymore, and that was what he needed. "What about him?"

"He and Philip are a package deal, and you know who his biological father is."

Abel glared at Eddie. "And what difference does it make? I'd never dream of separating him from Philip. Philip is a great father."

Eddie nodded. "I was just checking. I didn't think you were going to hurt either of them, but you know how it is. I feel like they're all my responsibility, at least in part. Joel would be there with them right now if we hadn't gotten married, and I hate that they have to hide to be safe."

"You're not the only one. And before you ask, yes, I see myself with Philip long term, possibly marriage-term. It's way too early to say, though. I have no idea how he sees me." Because no matter what Eddie had said, Abel hadn't noticed Philip watching him in a way that would betray deeper feelings. He wanted to believe it, though.

"You should romance him."

"What do you mean?"

"He's never had that. I know Oscar was the first man who touched him that way, and you know how that went. Philip has never known romance or love. He deserves to be treated well, like the treasure he is. So do it. Buy him flowers, something just for him and not for Myron. Make him feel loved for the man he is and not just the father and the friend."

That sounded good. Abel couldn't deny it did. That didn't mean he knew where to start, though.

He hadn't had time for a relationship in years. He hadn't looked for one. What he wanted with Philip felt fragile and delicate, and he knew he should work for it, show Philip that, as Eddie had said, there was more to him than a father and his past. He was always so hard on himself. Abel wanted him to forget the past and what had been done to him and focus on the future.

A future with him, hopefully.

Chapter Five

A bel didn't know what to do.

He'd come to Northwood specifically to find a nice gift for Philip, something that told him how much he meant to Abel, but what was he supposed to choose? There were so many things that looked nice and that Abel thought Philip would like. Which one would be more special to him?

Abel had spent some time watching Philip, as much as he didn't like to admit it. He'd been fascinated by Philip since the first time he'd laid eyes on him. He'd been frightened, dirty, and seven months pregnant, yet Abel had never seen anyone as beautiful as him. He wanted to convey that emotion through his gift, but he had no idea how to do that.

A book? Philip liked to read, although he mostly stuck to children's books these days. Abel supposed he didn't have a lot of free time to read fiction or whatever else he might like.

Flowers sounded nice, but they wouldn't last long, and they felt a bit impersonal.

Maybe a photo album with pictures of Philip and Myron? That would be personal enough, and Philip would like that, but it wasn't something Abel could buy today.

"I'd suggest a key to your place," a man said from behind Abel, startling him

Abel turned. "I'm sorry?"

The man grinned. "You're thinking about buying a gift for someone, right? You've been staring at this stuff without really seeing it." He waved at the display in the window of the shop Abel had stopped in front of. "It's obvious you want to find a good gift, so whoever it's for, he must be pretty important."

"And you guessed it was a *he*?"

The man laughed. "I had a fifty percent chance to get the right one."

Abel observed the man. He was on the short side, with short brown hair and hazel eyes. He looked harmless enough, but Abel thought he could see something in his eyes, and that something made him wary. "You guessed right." He offered the man his hand. "I'm Abel."

He was slightly surprised the man shook his hand. He'd expected him to decline. "Kari."

"I don't think I know you. Do I?"

"I've seen you around, but no, we've never talked. So? What are you going to buy?"

Abel sighed and eyed the window again. "I don't know."

"I still think the key to your house is a good idea."

It did sound like something Abel would be happy to do, but he wasn't sure how Philip would take it. Besides, Philip couldn't leave the Bishop house, and no one knew when he'd be able to.

"Or if you'd rather get something else, how about jewelry? Nothing expensive, just enough to tell him you care."

Abel had a hard time imagining Philip wearing something around his neck because Myron would latch onto it. A bracelet sounded nice, though, and there was a jewelry store a few shops over. "Thank you for your advice."

Kari didn't leave, though. No, he followed Abel to the jewelry store and even waited for him outside while Abel went to look at the bracelets. It made Abel uncomfortable, even though Kari hadn't done anything—not yet anyway. But Abel suspected Kari was there, talking with him, for a reason, and he wanted to find out what that reason was. He just hoped he wouldn't end up bleeding out in an alley somewhere.

Abel selected a thin leather bracelet. Since he could choose the small pendant that hung on it, he picked a tiny M. That way Myron would be there, but it was still mostly a gift for Philip.

He couldn't believe how nervous he was. The gift wasn't much, but it would be a visible mark of him on Philip if Philip accepted it and wore it. It wasn't quite the more permanent ring Abel wanted to put on Philip's finger, but they had a lot of road to travel before they could get to that part—if they ever did.

"It's cute," Kari said when Abel left the shop, the bracelet safe in a bag he was holding.

"What do you want? And don't say you just wanted to help, because I don't believe that."

"Well, I *did* want to help, although not in the way you're thinking." Kari pushed his hands into his jeans pocket and walked away. He hadn't told Abel to fuck off, so Abel followed him, berating himself for being an idiot. He was probably going to his death, and he was going willingly.

"So, your man," Kari said.

"Do you know Philip?" That would explain why Kari seemed so keen on helping Abel with the gift.

"I know *of* him. I know what happened to him. I know where he is, well, he and the others."

Abel froze. "What?" His voice sounded strangled.

Damn it. He wasn't the man for this situation. He knew Thomas and Morris would already have threatened Kari or got some answers out of him. And there *he* was, unable to get more than a *what* out.

Kari stopped and faced Abel. He rocked back on his heels and smiled. "Don't worry. I don't mean him or any of the others any harm. I wouldn't have killed Oscar if I did."

Abel opened his mouth. No sound came out of it. He

cleared his throat and tried again. "What are you talking about?"

"I know the council is aware of the fact that Oscar's brakes had been tampered with. That's because *I* was the one who did it." His smile faded. "Oscar deserved to die. A lot of them do."

"Are you here to kill me?"

Kari shook his head. "Why would I? You're one of the good ones. I know about you and your friends, how you're trying to make things better for the carriers in the forest. That's why I killed Oscar. I'm trying to help, too."

"Who are you?"

"That's not important."

Abel disagreed, but he could see from Kari's expression he wouldn't get an answer to that. "What do you want?"

"I know you and your people are putting together a team to free the carriers."

How the hell did he know that? Abel didn't bother denying it, though. Whoever Kari was, he knew what he was talking about. "And?"

"I want to be on that team. I could be your team member. I know you haven't been able to find a deer shifter for it."

Abel was starting to wonder if Kari could become invisible or something. "I can't promise you anything, especially not after what you just told me about Oscar."

"You need to talk to the others. I understand, and it's fine with me. Tell them what I told you. I know I have to be approved by them, too, to be part of that team."

"I can't promise you they will."

"I know. I need to try, though."

Whatever the reason Kari had to be part of that team, Abel suspected it was important. Maybe he'd lost someone, a carrier, and he wanted to avenge him.

Abel wasn't sure what to think of Kari. He didn't look like

he could hurt a fly, but he'd killed Oscar. Abel believed that. Kari wasn't lying, and he was serious about working with the team that would go in to check on the carriers they'd just found out about.

He nodded. "All right. I'll ask, and I'll try to convince them it's a good idea." Even though he wasn't sure it was. "How do I contact you?"

"I'll contact you."

"You also have my number?"

Kari grinned. "I have my ways. Thank you, Abel. And you really should tell Philip you love him. He loves you too, and he deserves to be happy."

Abel made a strangled sound. Of course Kari knew about that, too. "How do you know he'd be happy with me?"

"Like I said, you're a good man. It's obvious you care for him and that you'll do what you can to make him happy."

"You've been observing me." And probably everyone else, including the Bishop house.

"I have."

"Why?" Abel didn't think it was to hurt any of them. Kari had had the opportunity to do that if he'd been observing them, yet he hadn't. He hadn't even let himself be seen until now.

"Because I needed to know you were the good guys."

Philip heard the car stop in front of the house. He peeked through the window, smiling when he saw it was Abel's car. He wasn't sure how they'd left things the night before, but he felt like they'd taken a step forward and were closer to becoming whatever it was they'd be in the future.

Yesterday afternoon had been incredible. They hadn't done anything except spending time with Myron and talking, but Philip would give just about anything to do it again.

Maybe that was why Abel was here today. Or was he coming to have lunch like they'd talked about? Philip had thought he'd call first, but it wasn't like he had an abundance of things to do.

Philip turned to the crib. Myron was awake and cooing at the toys that hung over him. "Hey, baby. Want to go find Abel?"

Philip didn't get an answer—of course he didn't—but he thought Myron would be happy to see Abel. He always was.

He checked Myron's diaper, then headed downstairs with him. Abel was in the entrance, pacing back and forth. That was enough to tell Philip something was wrong, and the expression on Abel's face and the way he kept raking his hand through his hair solidified that impression. "Abel?"

Abel jerked. "Philip. I didn't hear you coming down."

"What's wrong?" Abel hesitated, and Philip knew what he was going to do before he did it. "Don't say *nothing*, because I can see it's not true. Did something happen?" Philip held Myron closer. "Are we in danger?"

Abel's shoulders slumped. "I'll be honest—I'm not sure, but I don't think so."

"Do we need to leave?"

"No. I called Thomas, and he's calling everyone else for an emergency meeting. Thomas wanted to have it at his house, but I needed to see you and make sure you were okay."

"I am. We both are." Philip wanted to push, but he could tell Abel needed all his attention. "Wait here. I'll find someone who can keep Myron for a bit so we can talk."

"You don't need to do that."

"Yes, I do. It's obvious you're shaken, and unless you really don't want to talk to me about it, I'd like it if you did." Philip bit his lower lip. "I want to be here for you if you need me," he added, whispering. They'd never gone this way, but he hoped it was the right thing to say and do.

Abel sighed heavily. "Thank you. I *would* feel better if I could talk to you."

"I'm sure I'll find someone in the kitchen or the living room. Give me a moment."

Of course, for the first time since Philip had arrived at the Bishop house, the living room was empty. Jacob was in the kitchen, though, making coffee, and Philip rushed by his side. "I need you to keep Myron for a bit."

Jacob's eyes widened. "Myron? Wait, Philip, I can't—"

Philip pushed Myron into Jacob's arms. "I'll be close, but if you need anything, please ask Chris or anyone else. Myron ate not too long ago and his diaper is clean, so he shouldn't give you problems."

Jacob looked utterly lost with a baby in his arms. He stared down at Myron as if expecting him to try to bite him, or maybe to start projectile vomiting all over the place.

Philip rolled his eyes and went back to Abel. Jacob could easily find someone to help him. Everyone in the house had taken care of Myron at one time or another, especially right after his birth, while Philip recuperated. He'd be fine.

Abel was closing the front door when Philip got back to the entrance. Philip arched a brow, but Abel shook his head. "Where do you want to talk?" he asked instead of answering Philip's silent question.

"Is here okay? I know people can hear us, but they'll try not to, and I'd rather be close in case Jacob needs help with Myron. He looked like he didn't quite know what to do with him."

Abel smiled. It was brittle. "Here is okay. I suppose everyone is going to find out about this sooner or later anyway."

Philip sat on one of the benches lining the wall. He had to push a pile of books to the side, but there was enough space for both him and Abel.

Abel didn't sit, though. He started pacing again.

"You're worrying me."

"I'm not sure how to say this." He stopped in front of Philip, and Philip saw him take a deep breath. "I found out who killed Oscar. I'm sorry, Philip."

Philip blinked. "What are you sorry for?"

"I know you hated Oscar, but he was still Myron's—"

Philip raised a hand. "No. Don't say it. He *wasn't* Myron's anything. He was a sperm donor." No words had ever felt so right.

"Right. I'm sorry."

"It's all right. I hate that Myron will only have me, but it's better this way."

Abel frowned. "He won't only have you, Philip."

"Well, of course not. He has a lot of uncles who love him. But he'll only have one parent, one father, and I hope that won't, you know, create some kind of problem for him. But I'm *glad* Oscar is dead. I know he would have tried to get his hands on Myron if he wasn't, and that's not something I want to think about."

There was an odd expression on Abel's face. He looked like he was about to talk, but like he was also trying to stop himself. It scared Philip, because he still had no idea what Abel was there for, what had happened.

Then Abel crouched in front of Philip. He reached behind his back, and he offered Philip a small, long box. Philip stared at it. "Abel?" It couldn't be a ring—why would it be anyway—but it *did* look like it might contain jewelry of some kind.

Abel cleared his throat. "I know we're not—that we're friends. And that's okay. I don't need anything more from you. But hearing you talking about how Myron only has one father, well, it hurt me. I don't have any rights over him, and you can say no and tell me to leave, but I'd like to be more than an uncle to him. I want to take care of him, of the two of you. He doesn't *need* a second father, but I'd like him to have one, to have *me* if that's okay with you. You're his father, and that won't change. But I love him, and I want him to have everything, including what I can give him."

Philip couldn't breathe. It wasn't the love declaration he'd been hoping for, but it was close to it, even though Abel had focused on Myron. Abel knew Philip and Myron came to-gether, and that meant he was ready to deal with Philip and have him in his life. "And this?" Philip asked.

Abel's cheeks flushed. "It's just a little something for you. I thought of you when I saw it, and I wanted to do some-thing nice for you. I can take it back if you don't like it, or you can exchange it, although I'll have to go for you, since I bought this in Northwood and you can't leave the house. But we can find a way to make it work."

Abel was adorable all flustered. Philip had never seen him like this. Abel was always quiet, but it was a quiet strength. There was something about him that told the peo-ple he was with that they'd have a fight on their hands if they pushed for the wrong thing. Right now, though, Abel looked like he might bolt, and that told Philip how im-portant this was for him.

He took the box. He was curious, and he suspected he wouldn't have to ask for something else. For all that Abel was quiet and didn't ask questions, he was also observant. He no doubt knew what Philip liked and disliked. "Thank you. You didn't have to."

"I know I didn't. I *wanted* to do it, to do something nice for you."

"You're always nice to me." Philip opened the box and sucked in a breath at the sight of the bracelet. Abel *did* know what he liked. It was something he might have bought for himself if he'd been free to leave the house and go shopping. The leather was thin and smooth, and the tiny pendant connected the bracelet to Myron. "Thank you. It's beautiful."

Abel finally smiled. "I'm glad you like it."

"I *love* it."

Abel got up and rubbed his face. "Good. That's good. I needed something nice to happen today."

Philip leaned forward, the bracelet momentarily forgotten. "You said you know who killed Oscar."

Abel sighed. "I do."

Abel didn't think Philip would be hurt. His reaction to Abel's apology had been strong and exactly what Abel had expected from him. He wasn't afraid of Oscar anymore.

"Are you going to tell me who it was?"

"A man called Kari. I know nothing about him. He stopped me in Northwood today and told me he did it."

Philip was clutching the box with the bracelet. "Why did he do that?"

"He wants to be part of the team that will go into mink and opossum territory to check in on the carriers there."

"Why?"

"I don't know. He didn't say much. I hope we can get more information about him when he contacts me again, though."

"Contact you? He's going to contact you again?"

"Yes. He wants to know what we'll decide about the team. He seems to think he did a good thing killing Oscar, something that proves he can fit in with us."

"He *did* do a good thing."

"I know." As much as Abel hated the loss of life, everyone was better off with Oscar dead. Besides, it was their way of life. The humans outside the forest wouldn't intervene. They let the shifters deal with their criminals, and since they didn't have a big jail but rather smaller prisons in every territory, the worst crimes were punished with death. It was harsh, but it was life as shifters, no matter how much Abel hated it. He knew he was softer than most other shifters in that regard, and that was okay with him.

The front door opened. Both Abel and Philip jumped, but it was only Thomas. "What's going on?" he asked Abel.

Abel sighed. He wanted more time with Philip. "I'll tell you as soon as everyone is here. Do you know who's coming?"

"I got a few confirmations. Do I need to up security?"

"I doubt it would do any good." Kari had somehow managed to slip through, and security had already been upped when the carriers had started arriving at the Bishop house. Whoever he was, Kari had managed to get around it, and Abel suspected he might have been able to get into the house. Even if he hadn't, he'd observed them long enough that he knew Philip and what he liked, and that didn't sit well with Abel.

"I'm going to go get Myron," Philip said. He hesitated, looked at Thomas, then at Abel. "Come talk to me once the meeting is over?"

"Of course." Philip hadn't yet told Abel what he thought about Abel's suggestion of being in Myron's life as more than an uncle, and Abel was nervous. He thought Philip had been accepting enough when he'd explained, and he'd appeared touched by the bracelet, but somehow, that didn't make Abel feel better.

"Kitchen?" he asked Thomas.

"Why not? But you do know I have an office back home, right? We could have met there."

"I know. I needed to see Philip."

"Mmm. I see."

"Do you?"

"Probably not. Not until you tell me what's going on."

Abel needed something strong, but he settled for coffee. Jacob was in the kitchen when Abel and Thomas walked in, but he left as soon as he saw them, probably realizing something was happening by their expressions. The others arrived little by little, looking as worried as Abel felt. Not all of them were there—it would have brought too much attention to them and the cete, so they always tried to be not more than five or six. The alphas usually came and reported to their council members. Abel was the exception, but that was more because he enjoyed being with Philip every time he was at the Bishop house than because he needed to be there. Of course, Rod was grateful that he didn't have to drive back and forth, and Abel liked his alpha enough to leave him at home when he could.

"Talk," Thomas said when the kitchen was full.

Abel didn't take exception at his tone. He knew everyone was on edge. He hadn't told them what was happening, and they were anxious.

"I was in Northwood today. A man came up to me and told me he'd killed Oscar."

There was an explosion of voices, all of them either swearing or asking questions. Abel waited until everyone shut up again to continue. "His name is Kari, and no, I've never met him before. I don't know who he is or why he killed Oscar, except that he said Oscar deserved it."

Morris snorted. "That's not a secret. *Everyone* thinks Oscar deserved it."

"But not everyone tampered with his brakes. And that's not all. Kari has been observing us, including the carriers. He told me things about Philip that made my skin crawl."

"We need to move the carriers?" Thomas asked.

That was a hard question to answer. Abel's first instinct

would be to say yes, but that was because he panicked at the thought of anything happening to Philip. "I don't think so."

"Explain."

Abel rolled his eyes. "You don't have to give me one-word sentences, Thomas. I'm not one of your cete members. But I'll explain. Like I said, I don't know this Kari, but we talked. I don't think he wants to hurt anyone, or that he's going to use what he knows against us. Think about it. He knows about this place and the people who live there. He could have contacted anyone on the council to tell them. He could have blackmailed us. Instead, he killed Oscar, and the only thing he wants is a place on the team we're putting together."

"Why?"

"I don't know. He didn't tell me all his deepest secrets. I don't even have a phone number. But between this and Oscar's death, I think Kari has something against the council, or the part of it we're fighting against, anyway." Abel swallowed. "He could have killed me. You all know I'm not trained. I couldn't fight my way out of a wet paper bag. But he didn't even threaten me. He just asked for a chance to help."

Morris leaned back in his chair. "That sounds good, but how can we know we can trust him?"

"We don't."

"He could use the information he has against us. There has to be a reason he hasn't, and I don't think he will even if we tell him we don't want his help."

"What do you think, then? Should we trust him?"

How was Abel supposed to answer that question? What if he said no and Kari created trouble for them? Or what if he said yes and it was the wrong decision?

"Just follow your instincts," Thomas said. He was smiling, and Abel relaxed. He hadn't done anything wrong, and it wasn't like whatever his answer was, they'd do it. They needed to talk about it first.

"I think he has good intentions. I think he had a good reason to kill Oscar, and I'm not sorry he did. As I said, he could have hurt me or anyone in this house if he'd wanted to, yet he only observed us. It's creepy, but I don't think he's dangerous, not to us."

"I want to meet him."

Abel looked around. Almost everyone was nodding, and he was relieved. The decision wouldn't be just his. "I think that's a good idea."

"How do we ask him, though?"

"He said he'll contact me again. I'm ready to bet he's observing us, and even if he isn't, he has to know I came here and asked for a meeting right away. What he told me warranted that. He's probably going to contact me later today or tomorrow."

"Good. The sooner we deal with this, the sooner we can deal with the rest. Some of the people we want on the team have already arrived," Morris said.

The team would stay in sleuth territory. They didn't want anyone too close to the Bishop house. They trusted the team members—they wouldn't have been chosen otherwise—but there were already too many people coming and going. No one outside the cete probably knew, but it would be easy for a cete member to talk and for the news to spread.

"I'll tell him what we decided when I see him," Abel said.

"Do you think he'll have a problem with talking to us first?"

"I don't. He wouldn't have reached out if he didn't want contact with us, and he knows he'll have to deal with us if he makes the team."

Abel had no idea how this was going to end. He *did* think Kari wanted the same thing they did, but he had no way to be sure of it, and it was putting everyone's safety at risk—including Philip's.

Philip snatched Abel as soon as he left the kitchen. "We need to talk."

Abel chuckled tiredly. "About what?"

"Don't play the idiot. You know." Although Philip wasn't sure himself, he wanted to talk about what had happened to Abel today, but also about what Abel had told him. His mind was a mess of questions, and he didn't know where to start. "What did you all decide about the guy who told you he killed Oscar?" he asked as soon as they were in his bedroom.

He'd dragged Abel there, knowing it was the only place where they'd have privacy. Myron was with Kaspar, so Philip wasn't worried about him. Kaspar was steady and trustworthy. He'd take care of Myron as if he were his son.

Abel sat on the edge of the mattress. "They want to meet him."

"Is that a good idea?" Philip didn't know the guy, but he was wary of him. He'd be wary of anyone who accosted Abel in the middle of the street to tell him he'd killed Oscar. He didn't care about the killing Oscar bit, though. Hell, he'd thank this Kari the first time he saw him if he could.

Oscar would have made Philip's life hell if he'd still been alive. Even if he hadn't known where Philip was, he could have raised hell. He'd been there when Alex and the others had rescued Philip, so he'd known who had Philip. Philip still couldn't believe Oscar hadn't tried anything in the months between Philip's arrival at the Bishop house and Myron's birth.

He would have done everything he could to get Myron. The main reason he'd kept Philip in that small, cold cell and raped him was to have a son.

"I don't know. We have to talk to him, though. He didn't merely kill Oscar. He observed the house and the people who live here." Abel looked down. "He was actually the one who suggested I buy you jewelry."

Philip raised his hand and tugged at the bracelet. "Did he choose this?"

Abel's cheeks flushed. "You're wearing it."

"Of course I am. You bought it for me."

"I also chose it. Kari didn't have anything to do with that. But he knows a lot of things about the house and the carriers. He could have hurt us a while ago, yet he hasn't."

"What do you think it means?"

"That he needs something from us, or that we have the same enemies." He shook his head. "Can we talk about something else?"

Philip wanted to stay on this topic, even though they'd said everything there was to say about it. It would be easier than facing what he'd feared since he'd met Abel. It was time, though, and after receiving the bracelet, Philip had hope.

He licked his lips. "When you said you didn't want to be only an uncle to Myron . . ."

"I meant it. I love him."

Do you love me? Philip didn't ask. He was too afraid. "Everyone here loves him."

Abel's smile was hesitant. "I know. I want more than Myron in my life, though."

Philip swallowed. "What more?"

"You."

Philip's knees felt shaky. He leaned against the crib, needing a moment to gather his thoughts. "We're friends." Because maybe Abel didn't mean what he'd said the way Philip had taken it.

"I know we are. I want more, though. Just like I want more than just being Myron's uncle."

"Why?" That was the one thing Philip still didn't understand. He could accept that Abel loved him—they'd been friends for a while—but how could he want more? *Why* did he want it?

"Why not?" Abel got up. He came closer to Philip, but not too close, probably afraid Philip would freak out. "You're everything I could want from someone. You're brave. Strong. A good father. You're loving and gentle, and so very sweet. You deserve so much more than what life has given you until now, yet I've never heard you being bitter or angry."

"Oh, I am angry. Trust me."

"I know. What I was trying to say is that I don't care about the past. I know it shaped you to be the man you are today, but it doesn't change the way I feel about you."

There it was. The moment that would make or break this. Philip thought he knew what Abel was going to say, but he needed to be sure. "How do you feel about me, then? Because you've said a lot of nice things, but you haven't told me that yet."

"That's because it's scary."

"I know." But one of them was going to have to take that step, and Philip wasn't sure he could. He didn't want to risk losing this, not when he'd lost so much already.

"I'm in love with you, Philip. It doesn't mean you owe me anything or that I need anything from you. I just thought you should know. It's becoming hard to keep it a secret from you."

"You can stop now."

Abel smiled. "I know. It's all in the open now."

Philip hadn't missed the fact that he hadn't told Abel what he felt for him yet. He wasn't sure how to do this, but he knew he had to. He didn't have to be afraid anymore, because Abel felt the way he did. He wouldn't lose him for being in love with him. "I'm in love with you, too."

Abel laughed. "Thank God. I wasn't sure you felt the same way, or that you were going to tell me if you did."

Philip couldn't help but smile. "What's next, then? I don't exactly have experience in this." Was Abel going to want them to have sex? Sooner or later, they would, and while the idea intrigued Philip, it also terrified him. The only sex he knew was violent and humiliating.

Abel wasn't Oscar, and he'd never behave the way Oscar had. Philips' heart knew that, but his brain was still playing catch-up. His brain was the part of him that wanted to take things slow and to make sure Abel was there to stay, that he really was the good man he showed to the world. It wanted Philip to be cautious, and Philip knew that Abel's answer would help him make a decision. He wouldn't have fallen in love with Abel if Abel hadn't been a good man, but even good men did terrible things sometimes.

"You don't need to have experience. Besides, it's not like I have much of it, either. We'll take things as they come, as slow or as fast as you want."

"What about what you want?"

"What I want doesn't matter. I already feel lucky to have you in my life the way I've had you recently." Abel rubbed the back of his head. "I don't want to treat you like you might break, but I also realize that you have a past, one that's not easy to deal with. That's why I want you to call the shots here."

"As long as you tell me if you're uncomfortable with something."

Abel laughed. He looked lighter, as if some of the weight he'd been shouldering lately was gone. "I doubt anything you can do will make me uncomfortable, but all right. How about we take things slow and both promise to speak up if we need to?"

That sounded good, too good to be true. But Philip wasn't going to back down, not now that he had what he'd been yearning for, no matter how scary it was.

He'd been through scary. What had happened with Oscar had been terrifying. It wasn't the same kind of fear, but the feeling was there, and Philip refused to let it rule his life.

He leaned toward Abel. "I think I'm ready for a kiss."

Abel's smile was shy, but it was there, gorgeous and wonderful and everything Philip had imagined. "You are?"

"Yes. I've been thinking about this since almost the first day. I just never thought you'd want to kiss me, too."

"Why not?"

"I was pregnant with another man's baby, and you, well, you're protective of everyone here. I thought maybe you wouldn't want me because you'd feel like you were taking advantage, or because you thought I was, you know, used."

"Never. I don't see it like that, Philip. I don't care that Myron isn't my son by blood. You're his father, and *that's* what's important, both to me and to everyone else. No one is going to remember Oscar in ten years, but everyone is going to love Myron because of who he is and how he was raised."

Philip leaned even more forward. He had no idea what he was doing, but it couldn't be hard, could it? Kissing was a press of the lips, so that was what he did, feeling Abel's breath against his skin, smiling as their lips finally touched.

Abel sucked in a breath and held still, too still. Philip wrapped his arms around Abel's neck and held on. He trusted this man completely. He knew Abel wouldn't hurt him.

He was home, finally.

CHAPTER SIX

Abel shuffled, his gaze moving to the coffee shop door more often than he liked to think of. He was nervous, yet relieved that Kari had asked to meet him in a public place.

Abel had been stunned when he'd gotten the text. He hadn't given Kari his number, but he wasn't surprised the man had somehow managed to get it. With everything he knew, he had to have his way of finding out things.

"Good morning."

Abel jerked. For five minutes, he hadn't been looking at the door, and of course, that was when Kari had walked in. "Good morning." It felt odd to talk to him as if they were friends, especially with what Abel knew about him.

"I'm going to grab a coffee. I need caffeine first thing in the morning."

It was going on eleven, but Abel didn't point that out. Kari probably worked nights, planning murders and sabotaging cars.

And he shouldn't think that way, because it made him even more nervous to talk with the guy.

Kari looked harmless, though. Abel looked at him as he strode to the counter and ordered a coffee with enough caramel syrup to make his teeth rot in his mouth. He was wearing jeans and a t-shirt and looked like every other young man Abel knew. His short hair was messy, and he looked like he'd rolled out of bed just before leaving his house, wherever that was.

"I know you weren't staring at my ass," Kari said as he walked back to the table.

Dammit. Abel had been lost in his thoughts again. He needed to stop doing that, especially when he was with Kari. "I was thinking."

Kari flopped into the chair in front of Abel. "I know. You don't look at anyone but Philip that way."

"I want to ask how you know that, but I'm pretty sure I don't want to know the answer."

Kari laughed. "You probably don't, no. So, what did they say?"

Abel sighed. Straight to the point. He wasn't surprised. "They want to meet you."

He expected Kari to say no. Instead, Kari smiled. "All right. Do they have a preferred day and time? Or should I just show up at the house and see what happens?"

"You'd get shot. That's what would happen." Abel fingered his cup. "I know you mean well, or at least I hope so. But the people who live in the Bishop house are important to the people I work with and me. Popping out there from out of nowhere isn't going to make them like you. If anything, they'll freak out and kick your ass."

"They could try."

Since Abel didn't know anything about Kari, he decided not to underestimate him. It wouldn't do, especially not when he knew how dangerous Kari was. He didn't know if Kari could fight, but he wouldn't be surprised if the answer to that were yes. "We only want to protect them."

Kari nodded. "Good, because that's what I want, too. And justice for them, and for all the carriers who ever suffered because of their alphas and their council members."

There was something personal there, Abel could see it. But he knew asking would result in Kari closing off, so he didn't. If Kari became part of the team, they'd probably get to know each other. "We want the same thing, then."

"I guess. So they want to talk to me? That's all?"

"For now. I can't promise you everyone will agree to have you on that team. We don't know anything about you, not who you are, where you're from, or even what kind of shifter you are. We don't know if we can trust you."

"What do *you* think?"

"I honestly have no idea. My instinct tells me you can be trusted, but I'm probably the least important of the council members."

"I don't think you are. Do you already know who will take Oscar's place?"

"No. We're not the ones in charge of that, unfortunately."

"You need someone on your side in his place."

"We do. That's the only way we'll be able to get rid of that stupid law that was passed. The only way the carriers who live at the house will be free to go back to their lives."

"You did a good thing, allowing them to stay there."

"I didn't do anything. Since you know where the house is, you know the only reason the carriers are safe there is because Thomas Steele is keeping them safe."

Kari waved Abel's words away. "Maybe, but from what I know, you're all contributing and trying to make things better. The only thing you can't get around is Alpha Grimes, then?"

Abel narrowed his eyes. "It is, for now." He didn't like the way Kari was insisting on that. "You're not thinking about doing something, are you?"

"Me? What would I do?"

Abel wasn't fooled by Kari's wide-eyed stare. "Don't tamper with his brakes."

"I promise I won't. When am I meeting with you and your friends, then?"

"It was difficult to find a day when everyone could be

there, but that's the only way they'd have it. Five days from now, Thomas Steele's house. You'll be allowed in cete territory that evening. He'd rather have you not sneak around."

"Not like he can stop me if I do."

"I suppose not. But if you want to work with us, you have to show us you respect us."

Kari huffed. "Fine. I won't sneak in. But just so you know, I can defend myself if anyone tries to restrain me or lock me somewhere."

"I have no doubt you can."

Kari was planning something. Abel could tell, even though he didn't know him well. What could he do about it, though? He doubted Kari would listen to him even if he tried to stop him. He might be a council member, but something told him Kari didn't care about that.

Abel hoped he wasn't making a mistake, both by ignoring what Kari was up to and by inviting him to the meeting. But he hadn't been the only one who'd made that decision, and he knew Thomas. The alpha would have his house surrounded, and he'd make sure Kari didn't have even the slightest opportunity to go anywhere near the Bishop house.

Abel was still worried. Philip and Myron were there, as were the other carriers. One mistake could ruin everything — their lives, their budding relationship.

"I'm not going to hurt anyone," Kari said softly.

"I want to trust you."

"But you can't."

"Not when I don't know you or what you're planning. No one has ever heard about you, as far as I know. You're an enigma, and I don't like it. I don't like the thought of putting Philip and everyone else at risk."

Kari gulped down the rest of his coffee and got up. "You're not putting anyone at risk, not by letting me help. I'll show you, Council Member."

Abel was even more worried now that he'd heard the resolution in Kari's voice.

Philip bounced Myron on his knee, smiling at his son's laughter. At least he was doing something good by channeling his nervous energy into this. He'd have been pacing the room if he hadn't been trying to entertain Myron. As it was, he still felt restless, and he wasn't sure what to do about it.

The front door opened, and Philip snapped his head toward the entrance, but it was Redley coming in from a run.

"God, you're jumpy today. What's up?" Chris asked.

"Nothing."

"Yeah, right. If you bounce that knee any harder, Myron is going to end up splattered on the ceiling. I'm afraid for my nephew."

Philip couldn't help but smile. He liked hearing Chris and the others call Myron their nephew. Myron would have a big family that would do anything to keep him safe. It was what Philip had always wanted for himself and something he'd never had, at least not until now. "He'll have you to scrape him off."

Chris kissed the top of Myron's head. "Maybe, but that doesn't mean you have to let whatever's up with you affect him. What's going on?"

"Nothing," Philip repeated. He knew Chris didn't believe him, though. He sighed. "I'm just nervous."

"Why?" Chris flopped next to Philip on the couch and wiggled his fingers at Myron. "Oh, wait. Abel hasn't been around yet today, right?"

Philip's cheeks heated. "He hasn't."

"And you're what? Worried about him?"

"In part." Abel had texted Philip this morning to tell him he was meeting the *Kari* guy who'd killed Oscar. The thought made Philip nervous, even though Abel had promised he'd be careful and that he'd meet Kari in a public place.

"Whatever he's doing, he'll be fine. It's his job, you know. He wouldn't be a council member if he didn't know what he was doing."

"I know." But Kari was an unknown entity, something no one could predict. What if he decided to hurt Abel because Abel didn't give him what he wanted? Philip knew the alphas and council members wanted to meet him before welcoming him in the field, and he might not take that well. What then?

"You said you were only in part worried about him. What else is bugging you?" Chris asked.

Philip didn't want to answer that. He and Abel had talked only yesterday, and even though they'd kissed, things felt so fragile. They hadn't had the occasion to be together since then. Philip knew Abel wouldn't have said what he'd said if he didn't believe it and if he wasn't convinced of it, but was he really ready to accept Philip's fears and raising a child that wasn't his? No matter what Abel had said, everyone knew that Myron was Oscar's son, and Philip was afraid that would weigh too much on Abel's life.

"You're not going to answer, are you?" Chris asked.

"You didn't give me the time to answer."

"I can tell you won't, though. It's on your face. Has something happened between you and Abel?"

Philip's complexion betrayed him. He knew he was blushing, and he couldn't help but look away before Chris could see the truth of that in his gaze. Of course, looking away told Chris what he wanted to know.

"I knew it," he crowed. He leaned closer to Philip. "What happened? Did the two of you kiss? Did you sleep with him?"

Philips' cheeks were blazing. "I didn't sleep with him."

"But you *did* kiss him, didn't you? God, Philip, I'm so happy for you."

Philip was happy, too, but like always, he was trying not to let that happiness take over. He couldn't, not yet. "It was just a kiss," he said, even though it had been more than that. Abel had told him he was in love with him, and he'd admitted to the same.

"With Abel? I doubt that. If he kissed you, then it means something. *You* mean something to him. Everyone around here knows that. It's kind of obvious, you know."

"I know I've been obvious."

Chris snorted. "That's an understatement. But it's not only you. It's obvious Abel adores you. It's plain on his face every time he looks at you. He's not going to take advantage of you or hurt you, and he's going to be a great dad."

Philip's whole being yearned for that, but he needed to take a step back. He'd had time to think. "I can't saddle him with everything."

"Everything what, Philip?"

"Me. Myron."

Chris narrowed his eyes. "What do you mean?"

"Well, we both know I have . . . problems. I'm not over what Oscar did to me yet, and I don't want Abel to have to restrain himself." Just the thought made Philip's cheeks feel even hotter, and he wasn't sure that was physically possible. "I don't know what I can give him when it comes to, you know. The bedroom."

"Sex."

"Yes." Philip wasn't used to talking about this. He'd answered Arlene's questions a few times, but she was a healer, and while Chris was probably Philip's best friend, Philip had never been comfortable talking to him about it.

"I doubt Abel expects anything from you when it comes

to sex. He knows what you've been through, and if there's anyone who's going to make sure you take things as slow as you need them to be, it's him." Chris frowned. "And if he doesn't, I'll have a chat with him. I learned to defend myself when I was a kid, and I can kick his ass."

That startled a laugh out of Philip. "You don't need to do that. And I know he'll give me time." Abel had said he would, and Philip believed him. "But that doesn't mean it's fair to him. And what about Myron? He's Oscar's son. He's already here, and I don't think Abel had planned to be a father, especially not so suddenly. With everything that's been happening, I don't want to put too much on him. He already has a lot to worry about."

"But—"

"Philip."

Philip's eyes widened. He'd been listening to the door since this morning, so of course, Abel had arrived when he was distracted. Had he heard what Philip had just told Chris? His voice didn't sound angry, but it *was* uncompromising, and Philip wasn't sure what it meant.

He turned toward the entrance and smiled at Abel, who was standing in the door frame. "You're back. How did everything go?"

"Well. Can I talk to you for a moment?"

"Of course." Philip looked at Chris. "Can you keep Myron for a while?" He didn't have to ask to know Abel wanted him alone. He could tell.

"Of course I can."

Philip had expected Chris' enthusiasm. "Thank you. I'll be right back."

"You don't need to be. Myron and I will be fine."

"I know."

Chris leaned closer. "He's not going to hurt you," he whispered.

"I know that, too."

"Then go and clarify things with him. You need to. And I don't want to see you again until the two of you are officially dating or engaged."

Chris' words and his certainty didn't help as much as Philip wished it would. He knew what Abel had said the night before, and he believed all of it, but was it right to put all this on Abel's shoulders? To barge into his life with all the problems that followed him and Myron and to force Abel to deal with them?

Abel wasn't sure what to think about what he'd just heard. He and Philip had talked yesterday. They'd confessed the feelings for each other. So why was Philip doubting everything again?

Maybe he wasn't. Maybe he was just wary, hesitant, and Abel could understand that—and deal with it. He wanted Philip to know that they were together and that they'd be together for as long as Philip wanted it.

Philip followed him upstairs. Abel stopped when they got to the bedroom door. He didn't want to barge into Philip's room if Philip didn't want them there, but he also wanted them to talk in a private place where no one would hear them and stick their noses into the conversation. "Is it okay to speak in your room?"

"Of course it is."

Abel opened the door and walked it. The sun was still shining outside, and the window was open, letting in the scents coming from the woods. They mingled with Philip and Myron's scents. It made Philip's bedroom feel like home.

Abel closed the door behind Philip. He wasn't sure how to start this conversation. He hadn't thought they'd have it again considering what they'd told each other yesterday. "I told you I wanted to be Myron's father if you let me."

Philip paled slightly. "I know."

"Have you changed your mind, then? Is that why you told Chris you didn't want to do this?"

Philip sat onto the bed. "I didn't tell him I didn't. I *want* to be with you. I'm just not sure it's fair to you."

"Why wouldn't it be?"

"You heard what I said before, didn't you? You know why. You're already helping so much, working so much. You shouldn't also have to take care of a newborn, especially when Myron isn't your son. I know you think—"

"I wouldn't have told you I wanted both of you in my life if I didn't mean it." Abel stood in front of Philip. "I want you. I want Myron. I don't care if I have to get up four times a night because Myron is hungry or he's sick. I want to do this. I want to be his dad, but you have to want it just as much." Abel raked a hand through his hair. He needed this conversation to go well. "Did you change your mind?"

"No. I want you, too."

"Then what's the problem? We talked about this already. Did you not believe me? Because I can tell you hundreds of times, but if you don't trust me, I'm not sure what I can do."

Philip shook his head. "It's not that, I told you."

Abel knelt in front of him. He'd probably regret this position later, but he needed to be close to Philip. "All right. I'm going to repeat what I told you yesterday. I want you and Myron. You're one of the few things that make me happy right now. I realize it's not going to be easy to balance my professional life as a council member and taking care of a newborn, especially when we can't live together, but I'm ready to try. I *want* to try. Everything else is a mess, and no one knows how it's going to end. You and Myron are my rock in the storm, or at least, I want you to be."

He wasn't sure what he'd do if Philip couldn't deal with all this. He'd walk away because he'd have to, and he'd continue to work with the alphas and the other council members because carriers deserved to be free to fall in love and live their lives, but he'd be dead inside. He wanted Philip to be happy, though. He *needed* Philip to be happy, even if it wasn't with him.

"I love you." There, Abel had said it even though it was terrifying.

Philip's eyes widened, and his expression softened. "I knew it already, but hearing the words . . ." he murmured.

"I'll tell you as often as you need and want to hear them. I love you, Philip. I think I've loved you since the first time I saw you."

Philip chuckled. "I was huge."

"You were pregnant, and look at how perfect Myron is. You were beautiful, then and now. That's never going to change. It's not the only reason I love you, of course, but it was the first thing I noticed."

"That, and my stomach."

Abel smiled. "It *was* pretty impossible not to notice it." Abel sobered. "But, Philip, I need you to believe me when I tell you I know what I want and what I'm doing. I wouldn't tell you this if I didn't think we could be great together and that we can make it work. Whatever is out there waiting for us, whatever is going to happen with the council and Kari and everything else, we'll be stronger if we're together. *I* will be stronger if I have you to come back to."

Abel understood why Philip was hesitant, but he hoped Philip would realize there was nothing to fear. No matter how complicated things might get, Abel would be happy as long as they were together. They *would* make things work, no matter how hard it was.

Philip felt better, as if something had lifted from his chest. It was easier to breathe and to believe that he and Abel could have a future.

He'd believed Abel yesterday, but he hadn't been sure Abel had thought about everything being with Philip would imply. Philip should have trusted him, though. Abel didn't do much without thinking about the pros and the cons, and that included being with Philip and offering him a future he'd never imagined he'd have.

And he wanted more. He wanted everything with Abel, but he wasn't sure how to ask for it.

Philip cleared his throat. "Myron is fine for a bit," he said.

Abel frowned. "I know that. Do you want to go find him, though? We can go check on him."

"No. I know he's fine. I was saying that because it means that *we* are fine for a bit, too, and, you know, we just decided to be together. To be a couple."

Abel smiled. "We did."

Philip knew he was going to have to be explicit. Abel would never do anything to spook him or even just annoy him, and that meant he'd follow Philip's queues when it came to everything, just like he'd said—and that included sex, or perhaps, it was mostly about sex. "The only person I had sex with was Oscar."

Abel's smile disappeared, and it was as if it had never been there. "That wasn't sex. It was torture. Oscar wanted to have power over you and to humiliate you."

Philip couldn't deny that. He still thought about what Oscar had done to him too often, but taking care of Myron and spending time with his friends and with Abel had helped him to start looking forward rather than at the past. He knew it would take him years to fully get over it—if he ever even managed to—but his life was good, and thinking about

Oscar would ruin it. Philip wasn't ready for that to happen. He didn't want to give Oscar that power, especially now that he was dead. "All right, it wasn't sex. Can we not talk or even think about Oscar right now, though?"

Abel's fierce expression smoothed out. "Of course. What were you trying to say?"

Philip knew he didn't have the words to explain himself. He'd only blubber and say the wrong thing, and then they wouldn't have the chance to get where he was trying to get them.

Abel was still kneeling in front of Philip, and Philip knew it couldn't be a comfortable position. He took Abel's hand and pulled him up, but when Abel tried to move away once he was on his feet, Philip dragged him closer to the bed instead. Abel's eyes widened just before he dropped onto the mattress. He twisted to void falling on top of Philip, but Philip didn't give him time to get up or to ask him if he was okay or if he was sure.

He rolled Abel onto his back and climbed on top of him. He straddled Abel's groin, shivering when he felt Abel's cock hardening under his him.

"What are you doing?" Abel asked. His voice sounded strangled and a bit breathless, but also careful, as if he was afraid to spook Philip. He probably was, and Philip didn't blame him.

He still hoped Abel would be *less* careful with him, though. He supposed that would come in time, once they both learned how far and what Philip was ready for.

"We have a few hours without Myron," Philip said. "And since we're a couple now, I thought we could do things couples do."

Abel put tentative hands onto Philip's thighs. "I like that idea, but you know we don't *have* to do anything, all right? Whatever you feel ready for—"

"I know. You're not going to push. That's just not you."

"I would never forgive myself if I scared you. I never want you to be afraid of me."

"I'm not." If there was one thing Philip was sure of, it was that he would never be scared, not with Abel. He knew Abel was nothing like Oscar and that he'd never do something to hurt him.

"What do you want?" Abel asked softly.

"Can we do it like this?" Philip wasn't sure he liked being in control, but he also knew it would be the best position to make sure he didn't freak out.

"Of course. But maybe we could move up the bed? It would be more comfortable."

Philip's cheeks flushed. "Whatever you want. I'm not—"

"Used to this. I know, and I don't care. We agreed to talk if we needed something, remember? That hasn't changed." Abel hesitated. "I don't know how comfortable you are with nudity, so what do you want me to take off? Because if I'm under you, it will be easier to do it now, before we get settled."

"I want to see all of you." Oscar had never gotten naked with Philip, thank God. Like Abel had said, it hadn't been about sex but about power, and what Oscar had wanted—to get Philip pregnant. Once he'd managed that, he'd left Philip alone.

"You're sure?"

"If you're okay with it, yes." Philip wanted to associate sex—making love—with being comfortable with each other. He'd never seen anyone naked but himself and Myron, and this was such a different situation. The fact that Oscar had stayed mostly dressed helped, though.

Philip had to get up to let Abel move. He watched the man he'd fallen in love with remove his clothes hesitantly, and he didn't miss the way Abel sucked in his stomach and tried to position himself so that Philip would see him side-ways. It took Philip a moment to realize what was happening.

He sighed. He wasn't the only one with hang-ups, yet they'd only focused on his. "You didn't have to hide from me, Abel. I know it's more easily said than done, but I *like* your body. I like looking at it."

Abel shrugged, his cheeks red. "I know I'm not built like the guards around here or most of you guys."

"So what? That doesn't change the fact that I like how you look. I mean, should I hide from you because I think I'm too thin and I have scars?"

Abel's eyes widened. "No! I'm sure I'll love your body. I love *you*. All of you."

"The same goes for me." Philip knew it would take Abel a little while to get used to the idea and to become comforta-ble, but he didn't mind. They both had to learn to be togeth-er and to leave the rest of the world, including their hang-ups, outside the door.

Abel stopped sucking his stomach in as he moved back onto the bed, but he *did* shield his cock with his hands. It didn't last long, because he was hard and they both knew what they were about to do. Philip wasn't sure what he'd be comfortable doing and taking off, so he just dropped his jeans and kept on his t-shirt and his boxer-briefs. He could always take them off if he felt comfortable enough.

He climbed back on top of Abel, who had to let his cock go. It sprang up, pushing against Philip's groin. Philip wasn't sure how to sit so they'd both be comfortable. He wasn't sure sitting *on* it would imply something he wasn't ready for, so he kept it between them, pressed against his own. He was hard in his underwear, and the contact felt good—and he was still half dressed. He could only imagine what things would be like when they both got naked.

He pressed forward, kissing Abel until they both relaxed. Abel's touch was light but firm, keeping Philip in the moment. Philip focused on Abel and how he felt against him— hands stroking down his back and under his t-shirt, hairy thighs prickling Philip's skin where he sat on them, soft stomach pushing against Philip's, their cocks brushing against each other with every move they made. The urgency was building with every kiss, every stroke of Abel's hands on Philip skin. Philip didn't want to get more naked, yet he wanted to. Most of all, he wanted to come and to see Abel come, to *feel* it. It was a new sensation, a new craving, but he was ready to experience it.

Philip bit his lower lip. He had no idea what he was doing, so it would probably be better to act on instinct. He knew what his body wanted.

He pushed his boxer-briefs down enough to free his cock. It bumped against Abel's, and they both sucked in a breath. Philip was still hesitant as he wrapped his hands around both of them. He had to let go with one hand to hold onto Abel's shoulder, but Abel replaced it with his own, twining their fingers together as much as possible in that position and rubbing his thumb over the head of Philip's cock.

Pleasure exploded. It ran down Philip's back, making him whine and lean more heavily into Abel. Their lips found each other's. They weren't really kissing, not anymore, not when Philip was panting as if he'd been running a marathon, but it felt so good, and Philip was so close to Abel like this.

Philip's thighs trembled as he finally reached the peak. He wanted to wait for Abel, to help him get there too, but he couldn't think about anything that wasn't the pleasure coursing through him and finally exploding from his cock. He tensed as he came, throwing his head back slightly because he needed to breathe. He could hear Abel whine and feel him push up, moving his hips until he too came, his cum joining Philip's on Philip's t-shirt.

Philip didn't even care that he'd have to change and probably shower. Hopefully, this was the first of many times.

CHAPTER SEVEN

Philip had never felt so warm in his bed. He was in that moment between sleep and being awake, that moment where things could go either way. He wasn't sure what had woken him until he heard Myron shuffle in his crib.

Philip didn't move, not yet. He let himself enjoy the weight next to him on the mattress, the way Abel's arm was slung around his hip, pulling him close. Philip was the taller between them, but he was the little spoon right now, neatly tucked against Abel's front. Their legs were tangled, and it felt so good to be this close to the man he loved. He never wanted it to end.

But it was going to, because Myron was about to wake up. He was no doubt hungry, and while Philip couldn't wait for a time when he wouldn't have to wake up in the first hours of the morning to feed his son, he also cherished the moments it gave them. The rest of the house was asleep, and the world was muted. Philip never turned on lights, so as to not have Myron think it was time to play, so everything stayed soft.

The noises from Myron's crib became stronger, and Philip sighed. He needed to get up before Myron would wake Abel.

He moved forward, raising Abel's arm, but it tightened around him, and Abel kissed the back of his neck. "Stay in bed. I'll take care of him," Abel said, shocking Philip into stillness.

Philip hadn't even thought this might happen. He was so

used to taking care of Myron alone, at least during the night, that the fact that Abel was ready to get up and do it for him stunned him. "I can go. I'm used to it."

Abel kissed Philip again, and Philip could feel his smile. "I know. I *want* to do it."

"Are you sure? You have to get up early to go to work tomorrow."

"I'm sure."

Philip briefly wondered if he was crazy, because who wanted to get up at night to feed a newborn? But as Abel slid out of bed, he realized that Abel probably had the same reasons he had. They both loved Myron, and they both knew it had to be done. They both saw it as their responsibility.

Abel had already snuck his way into Philip and Myron's life, and it felt as if he belonged there.

"Hey there, baby," Abel murmured. He soothed Myron, and Philip listened to both of them. He listened to Abel as he changed his son, as he got his bottle ready and as he sat in the chair next to the window to feed him.

It was odd not to be the one doing that, and one more weight lifted from Philip's chest. He wasn't alone anymore. He'd never have to cry alone while feeding his son because he was afraid he wasn't worth it, that he couldn't do it on his own. He didn't *have* to do it on his own, not anymore.

He didn't fall asleep again, listening to Abel move in the dark room. He wasn't sure he *could* sleep, not when his heart felt so full and about to explode. When Abel slipped back into the bed, Philip rolled toward him. "Thank you," he murmured. He could hear Myron shuffling still, and he knew they had to be quiet, because he'd wake up entirely otherwise.

Abel smiled and kissed the tip of Philip's nose. "You have nothing to thank me for. I told you I wanted to be with you, and that means taking care of both you and Myron. I'm happy to do it."

Philip knew that was true. It would have been easy for Abel to stay in bed and let Philip get up, yet he hadn't, even though he'd have to get up early to leave and go to work.

Philip sighed and snuggled closer to Abel. He wanted this every night, for the rest of his life. "I'm glad you're here."

Abel kissed Philip's hair. "I wouldn't want to be anywhere else."

But he'd have to, sooner or later. No matter how good this felt, or that they'd decided to be together, Abel was a council member, and the deer herd wasn't close by. Philip was surprised Abel had been at the Bishop house as often as he had lately, and he knew it had to be because of him. It would eventually start weighing on Abel, though, especially with everything else that was happening. Abel had to meet with the rest of the council and find a solution to the problems the people in the forest had, the biggest of which was finding a way to convince Alpha Grimes to appoint someone decent to take Oscar's place in the council. Abel couldn't do anything if he stayed at the Bishop house with Philip and Myron.

Maybe once the law that said that all unmarried carriers had to be handed off to the council was voted away, Philp and Abel could be open about their relationship. Philip wanted to hope, but he didn't dare to, not when Myron was Oscar's son. It would be too easy for Alpha Grimes to take Myron away from Philip by saying he only wanted the best for him and that being Oscar's son, he deserved to grow up with Oscar's family. They were as rotten as Oscar had been, and Philip would die before he let any of them touch his son.

So it would be better for them to stay hidden. Philip didn't know for how long and whether he'd have to get married to be free again, and he didn't want to think about it just yet. There was time, still, and he wanted to focus on Abel and their new relationship.

They were becoming a family, something Philip didn't feel he'd ever had. *That* was the only thing worth focusing on. His problems weren't going anywhere, and he couldn't do anything to solve them. He could love and support Abel, though. He *would* love and support Abel, always.

CHAPTER EIGHT

Abel couldn't stop smiling. Even though he wasn't at the Bishop house with Philip like he wanted to be, he hadn't been able to stop the stupid grin from forming on his face since the night he'd spent there a few days ago. He wasn't sure he *could*, not when he kept thinking about Philip, about how they'd woken up in each other's arms, how they'd cuddled for a bit before Myron had stirred. About how after Myron had been fed, they'd snuggled back under the covers with him between them.

It felt like Abel had a family now. It wasn't something he'd imagined for himself, but he loved it, and he couldn't wait to go back.

He glared at the pile of files on his desk. There was a lot of work to do as a council member. Sometimes, he wished he hadn't accepted Rod's decision to nominate him, but he hadn't had anything better to do back then. He did now, but of course he couldn't stop being a council member. His job was even more critical now that he had to keep Philip and Myron safe. Reading up on disputes between the bats and the raccoons wasn't going to do much for that, but it was work anyway, and Abel couldn't refuse to do it.

He was happy when his phone rang, though. He thought it was Philip and answered without looking at the screen, his gaze still on the file in front of him. "Please tell me you're saving me from these files," he begged.

There was a pause. "Abel."

Abel frowned. "Calder? Is everything okay?" They both

knew what he meant by asking that—*who* he meant.

"Yes, yes. I'm not calling because of him or anyone living there. Don't worry."

Abel leaned back in his chair. "But someone *is* hurt."

"Yeah. Well, dead. Alpha Grimes."

Abel blinked. This wasn't something he'd expected. "Alpha Grimes is dead?"

"Yes. They found him this morning in his office. Looks like a heart attack."

Abel wanted to believe that. "*Looks* like?"

"We won't know more until the coroner can examine him, of course, but as far as I know, there weren't any signs of violence. I doubt the prickle would have kept quiet if that was the case, especially after Oscar."

"But the fact that it looked like a heart attack doesn't mean it was one."

"No, it doesn't. Who would want to kill both Oscar and Grimes, though? Well, apart from us. Grimes hadn't yet chosen a new council member, had he?"

"No, he hadn't." But Abel could too easily think about who might have killed him, if that was what had happened.

Kari hadn't been happy about Grimes. Abel couldn't remember which of them had brought him up in their conversation, but he knew he'd explained to Kari that Grimes would be the one appointing the new council member and that they couldn't do anything about it. Had Kari taken that as a suggestion to get rid of Grimes?

Abel wouldn't be surprised, not with the way Kari had taken care of Oscar and how normal he seemed to think it was.

"Well, I just wanted to let you know. You wouldn't happen to have an idea about who the next alpha might be?" Calder sighed. "God, this is a mess. Remind me why I accepted this job?"

Abel chuckled. "I was just wondering the same thing. Probably because we want to do some good."

"Yeah. Well, I hope we'll manage now that Grimes is out of the way. I'm just not sure that killing all the people that stand between us and what we need to do is a good idea."

"I can't say I'm sorry either of those men are dead, but I get where you're coming from. And no, I don't know who will be next. Did Grimes have a son?"

"My next step is to contact my PA and have him look at the files. I'm in cete territory right now, so I can't do it myself. I'll let you know, though."

"Thanks." But Abel had a faster way to find out, and it wouldn't be a hardship.

He'd never say no to a trip to the Bishop house.

He called Rod on his way out to let him know what had happened and where he was going. His alpha never questioned his movements, but they were living in dangerous times, apparently, so he wanted Rod to know where he was, just in case. He suspected Kari had something to do with Grimes' death, but he had no way of contacting the man, and the meeting with him was still a few days away. Abel couldn't ask him, and he didn't know Kari well, but it would fit with him. Was he trying to show Abel and the others that he deserved a spot on the team? How had he managed to get into porcupine territory and kill Grimes and make it look like a heart attack? Or had it *really* been a heart attack?

Abel didn't believe in coincidences, not when they were this big. He hoped Grimes' death had been natural, but he knew better. That wasn't the most important thing, though. Now that Grimes was out of the way, Abel and the others needed the next alpha to be someone decent. He hated sticking his nose into anyone's business—that wasn't why he'd accepted the job as a council member—but this was what the forest needed. The shifters who lived there had been divided for too long. Too many of them weren't allowed a normal, decent life just because of what they were and what they could do. They'd been subjected to the will of the people who should have kept them safe and hadn't, and Abel didn't want that to happen again.

Philip had suffered in a way that shouldn't have happened, all because of the two men who were dead. More people would suffer if the next porcupine alpha was like Grimes. Abel needed to do something. He wasn't sure what, though. This wasn't something the council had a say in. Alphas and how they were chosen were family things. Only porcupine shifters would have a say in it. It made sense, and Abel didn't think it needed to change, but in this case, it could ruin him and the people he was working with. It could make everything they were working toward crumble, and it could destroy the lives of the men living in the Bishop house.

Including Philip.

Philip squeezed the toy, making it squeak. Myron's eyes widened, and he laughed. Something in Philip's heart fluttered. He'd never realized just how much he'd love his son until Myron was born. He'd loved his daughter, too, but she'd been taken from him before she was big enough to survive outside of him. It hadn't been the same. Myron was growing up with Philip, spending every day with him, learning things and becoming a person right in front of Philip's eyes.

"Philip? Why is your man here at this hour of the day?" Gail, one of the badger guards, asked from where she was sitting by the living room window.

Philip flushed. He and Abel hadn't officially declared they were together, not to the people Philip lived with, but they all knew. They'd seen Abel the morning after the night he and Philip had spent together, and word had spread. Abel hadn't been in a hurry to go home or to sneak out, and he'd had breakfast with them, feeding Myron as Philip made pancakes for everyone. He'd looked at home, and when he'd left, he'd kissed Philip and Myron in front of everyone.

So there was no hiding they were together now, and Philip was happy about that. He didn't *want* to hide it, even though he knew it might complicate things for Abel. No one in the Bishop house cared or would use it against Abel, but the people outside might. That was one of the reasons Philip had been hesitant, but there was no denying he and Abel loved each other, no stepping back.

He peered out the window. "I have no idea. He didn't call me."

Gail grinned. "So it's a surprise? How sweet."

Philip blushed. "He is, isn't he?"

Gail grinned. "You got a good one there, Philip."

Philip knew that. It was hard to believe he'd managed to fall in love with someone like Abel when he'd barely left Bishop house since he'd arrived. Maybe it was the way life had found to apologize for what he'd gone through with Oscar. If so, it had been worth it. Philip would forget what Oscar had done to him over time, but he'd never forget Abel and the love they shared.

Philip put down the toy and took Myron in his arms. He went to greet Abel at the door, smiling in spite of himself. He couldn't have stopped even if he'd wanted to. He was too happy.

Abel smiled back when he opened the door and found Philip there, but Philip could tell something was wrong. It was written all over Abel's face. "What happened?" he asked. He wished he could believe Abel was there because he'd missed him, but there was something else.

Abel sighed. "Let's go to your bedroom."

Philip's heart was racing as he climbed the stairs. He could too easily imagine what was wrong—someone had found out about him and Abel, someone had found out about the house, Alpha Grimes had something up his sleeve, or maybe he'd picked a worse council member than Oscar.

"Alpha Grimes is dead," Abel said as soon as the bedroom door was closed behind them.

Philip froze. That wasn't what he'd expected to hear. "What happened to him?"

"As far as we can tell, heart attack, but the porcupines are taking care of it, and you know how that goes. We'll only find out what they want us to find out."

Philip put Myron in his crib and turned on the mobile so he'd be entertained for a while. "Can't the council ask for details?"

"We will." Abel sat on the bed and rubbed his face. "But I suspect the heart attack thing is only a show. How much of a coincidence can this be? If I didn't know you'd never do something like this, I'd suspect you killed both Oscar and Grimes."

"What about Kari?" Because if he'd had a reason to kill Oscar, then it wasn't much of a stretch for him to have a reason to kill Alpha Grimes, too.

"I don't know. I think he might have something to do with it. We're meeting him in a few days, so I wouldn't be surprised if he'd done this to impress us. We briefly talked about it when we met, so no, I wouldn't be surprised. I'm not sure how he managed to make it look like a heart attack and why he hasn't contacted me to tell me about it."

"You still have no idea who he is?" Kari sounded like he'd trained to do this, and it wasn't a skill a lot of people in the forest had and could teach.

"No. No one I've contacted has ever heard of him. It's like

he appeared out of thin air the day he killed Oscar. I still don't even know what kind of shifter he is. That would help narrow things down and give me a direction. But I doubt I'll find out anything unless he wants me to."

Philip sat next to Abel. "What now?"

"Are you okay? This kind of news isn't easy to deal with."

Philip thought about it. Alpha Grimes hadn't hurt him the way Oscar had, but he'd been complicit. He'd allowed Oscar to take Philip away from his family and lock him up in a cell on his own. He'd let Oscar rape Philip, kill his unborn daughter, and get him pregnant again, without doing anything to help Philip. Philip had no doubt he'd have also let Oscar take Myron away when he was born if he'd still been in prickle territory when it had happened.

Alpha Grimes had hurt Philip in a different way than Oscar, but he'd hurt him nonetheless, and Philip couldn't forgive that. "I'm okay."

"You're sure?"

"Yes. I can't say I'm happy he's dead, but I'm also not sorry. He might never have touched me the way Oscar did, but that's what he was planning to do to Vincent. He was just as bad, and the world is better without him in it."

"What about the prickle, though? Grimes was an asshole, but the prickle doesn't have an alpha now. Did he have an heir?" Abel asked.

"No. He only had daughters." Which was probably one of the reasons he'd decided he wanted Vincent. The thought made Philip's skin crawl.

"So the beta."

"I hope not."

Abel took Philip's hand and twined their fingers together. "Is he as bad as Grimes and Oscar?"

"Maybe not as bad, but he's not a nice man either. I realize that most people in the prickle probably didn't speak up because they were afraid, including him. But he *liked* watching. He was there when Alpha Grimes and Oscar came to take me away from my home. I could see he liked it. He's not going to be a good alpha." But there wasn't another possibility. The prickle was so very traditional when it came to these things. Beta Thomason was the only man who could take the alpha's place.

"Who would you choose as the next alpha if you had a say in it?" Abel asked.

That was easy to answer. "Alpha Grimes' daughter, or maybe her husband if she can't be selected."

"Oh?"

"We weren't friends. I didn't have friends, not once people realized what I was. But she's not a bad person. She sometimes spoke up to her father, even though she never managed to change his mind. She knows wrong from right, though, and she won't be a bad alpha. Besides, isn't this what you and the others are trying to do? To finally get the shifters in the forest to leave some of our stupid traditions behind, like the one that says that Chris can't be an alpha because he's a carrier? That should go for women, too. I'm not saying all women are good people, but I've mostly been hurt by men. Changing this wouldn't be a bad thing."

Abel smiled. "You've thought about this a lot, haven't you?"

Philip had a lot of time to think when he was still in the cell Oscar had put him in. "I have. I think the traditions, both when it comes to who can be the alpha and the carriers, are wrong, and that they're hurting people. Being a carrier doesn't mean Chris can't be a good alpha. If anything, he'll understand how to treat people better because of how he's been treated. It's not fair that he shouldn't take his father's place if that's what he wants and if he's good at it. And think about Myron. What if he's a carrier, too? Don't you want him to have all the possibilities in the world when he grows up? I want my son to be whatever he wants to be, whatever he is."

Philip didn't care much about himself, but he'd fight to the death when it came to his son.

Abel loved how passionate Philip was about this. He loved Philip, period, and everything he was, his memories and his experiences, the future they were going to share.

"I want to do the right thing," he said, "But I don't know if the prickle will agree."

Philip shrugged. "Maybe not. *Definitely* not when it comes to the elders. They're the ones who are the most attached to traditions."

"Because it serves them."

"Yes. They're not going to be happy. They're going to resist. As is Beta Robertson, because you'd take his chance at being the next alpha from him. But he's not the best thing for the prickle. I know that. Everyone in the prickle knows it, but they're not going to be able to do anything about it. They're too scared."

"I'd like you to come to one of our meetings again." Abel could explain what Philip had just told him, but Philip would do a better job. He knew what he was talking about. He'd spent all his life with the prickle. He was passionate about this, and that was what they needed.

Philip's shoulders slumped. "That's what I thought you might say. You can't tell the others about this yourself?"

"I could, but I think they need to hear it from you. No matter how much you might hate the prickle, it was still your home until a few months ago. You, better than anyone in our group, knows what the prickle is like and what they need. You know every player in this game. If we want to have a new porcupine council member who's on our side, we need the next alpha to be a good one. It will be good both for us and for the prickle. I know you don't like the people who live there after what they did to you, but I know you. I know that no matter your feelings for them, you won't allow them to be hurt."

Philip squeezed Abel's hand. "You have so much faith in me."

"Of course I do. I know you. Anyone would be afraid and bitter in your place. And maybe you are, but you manage to get over it, to work things through and think about what would be best. You might not go back to the prickle, but think about it. What if you do?" Abel had no intention of letting Philip go. He knew Philip didn't want to go back to the prickle, and if Abel and the others managed to get the laws changed, he wouldn't have to.

"I'd rather stay here," Philip muttered.

"I know, and you can stay here for as long as you want, even after this mess is over. Thomas will no doubt make you a cete member, if that's what you want." But Abel hoped Philip would one day become a herd member and his husband. It was too soon to suggest something like that, though, no matter how much he wanted to. He didn't want to spook Philip, and pushing too much too soon would do just that. They were in a good place right now, and that was all that mattered.

"I don't know what I want from the future beyond making sure that Myron is safe and can have a happy childhood and life."

"You have time to think about it and decide."

Philip leaned against Abel's side. "I do, and I have you. I want you to be part of that future, too. You're Myron's dad, after all."

Abel was pretty sure his heart stopped at those words.

They'd talked about it, but it was such a difficult thing to wrap his mind around, especially with Myron being so young.

He was a father now. Even though they didn't live together, even though Abel had to spend too much time away from his family, Philip and Myron were it for him. They were his present and his future.

Maybe mentioning that he wanted to marry Philip wasn't a bad idea after all. They'd celebrated a few weddings already recently—Joel and Eddie's, Seamus and Alex's—so what would be one more? Both Abel and Philip were serious about this. They both understood how serious this was, and they were in this forever. Being married wouldn't change that. If anything, it would keep Philip safer because he wouldn't be as vulnerable. No one would be able to use his unmarried status as a carrier against him.

Because if they didn't manage to get that law changed, that was what would happen. The other half of the council would demand Philip be handed off if they ever found out about him. Myron would no doubt be given to the prickle, separated from his father, the one person who loved him the most in the world. But if Philip and Abel were married, no one would be able to touch Philip. They wouldn't have an excuse to do it.

And that wasn't the only reason Abel and Philip would be married. They loved each other, and they loved Myron. They were a family. *That* was the main reason Abel wanted to marry Philip. If it also helped to keep him safe, he wasn't going to complain.

But that was a conversation for another day. Right now, they needed to focus on what was happening with the prickle. Philip wouldn't leave the Bishop house until it was safe, and Abel trusted Thomas and the guards to make sure no one found out about it or managed to get to it.

Abel brushed the knuckles of his free hand along Philip's cheekbone. "I promise you'll be safe. You know that. The meeting can be held here again, so you won't have to leave the house or to be away from Myron for too long. I'll stick with you the entire time, and you know the people who will be there. None of them will hurt you."

"I know that, and I'm not afraid of them. I just wish I didn't have to talk about the prickle and Alpha Grimes. I never wanted to think about those things again, yet I have to."

"I know. But the forest will be safer for everyone if we manage to influence who the next alpha and the next council member will be."

"That's the only reason I'm agreeing to it. I want Myron to be safe. I want my friends to be safe and to be able to marry who they want and do what they want in life. And I want the people who hurt me to pay. That will only happen if the next alpha is a good, fair one. I'm ready to talk for that."

Abel pulled Philip close and kissed his cheek. Being able to touch him like this still stunned him, and he wanted to take advantage of it every time he could. The casual kisses and touches were some of the best ones, especially when they came from Philip. It was like he was getting used to Abel's presence in his life and acted without thinking about it. It meant he was comfortable with Abel.

Philip sighed and snuggled close to Abel. He had to stoop a bit since Abel was shorter, but even like this, they fit together.

"Everything is going to be okay," Abel murmured even though he couldn't make that promise.

"I hope so."

CHAPTER NINE

Philip bit his thumbnail and stared out the window. He could see the cars of the people who were there for the meeting. They were talking downstairs, moving around. He didn't want to join them, and he wouldn't, not until Abel was there.

Abel had managed to organize everything in just one day. He'd left yesterday evening even though they'd both wanted him to stay. Philip wished they could spend every night together, and not just because Abel didn't have a problem getting up to feed Myron, although Philip loved watching them together. He missed Abel when he wasn't there, and he wanted to spend more time with him. That was probably normal, since their relationship was so new, but Philip wanted them to start their new life together, whatever that meant. He wanted their lives to be normal, not for him to have to hide and to have to be away from Abel because it could be dangerous.

A knock on the door made Philip jerk. He knew it wasn't Abel—his car wasn't parked in front of the house yet—and he hoped it wouldn't be someone asking him to come downstairs to start without Abel. Philip wasn't sure he could do that, even though everyone in the meeting would be a friend, somewhat.

It was Joel. Philip relaxed when he saw him and stepped aside to let him in. "What are you doing here?" Joel often visited the Bishop house. He and his husband liked to bring the carriers things they couldn't get their hands on since they were stuck in the house. They made sure life in the Bishop house was as non-frustrating as it could be, although that wasn't easy. There were ten of them living there now, all with their own personalities and needs.

Joel made a beeline for the crib, where Myron was sleeping. "I volunteered to watch the little bug while you're in the meeting."

"Oh. You don't have to do that. Chris said he would."

"I know, but I missed Myron, and I'm sure Chris wouldn't mind spending some time with Jacob, since he's not working right now."

"He could have told me."

"He could have, but everyone wants to be with Myron. He's so cute, and an absolute angel."

Philip chuckled. "Especially when he's sleeping." Philip swallowed. It was easy to joke around, but his thoughts couldn't wander far from what was happening. He wouldn't have to leave the house today, and probably tomorrow either, but he knew it would happen soon.

He'd had the to think about it. The prickle wouldn't be happy, and if there was anything he could do to help Abel and his friends, he would — even if it meant leaving the Bishop house and his son behind. "If anything happens to me . . ." he started, but he couldn't finish.

Joel's eyes widened. "What? Is something wrong? Why should something happen to you?"

"Why shouldn't it? Everything is a mess right now, and even though we're relatively safe here, it doesn't mean we always will be. I just want you to know that if something happened to me, I want Abel to raise Myron, and if he can't, I want you and Eddie to do it." He'd have chosen Chris, who was his best friend, but Chris would have plenty of things to focus on, and Philip didn't want to burden him.

"Nothing is going to happen to you, Philip."

"I know. But I hate not knowing what's going on, and it's not like people keep me in the loop. Abel does, but he doesn't know everything himself. I want to be sure everything is covered, just in case. It would make me feel better."

Joel sighed. "I can understand that, unfortunately. All right. If anything happens to you, and it won't because no one here will allow it, I'll make sure Abel raises Myron or I'll do it with Eddie if he can't. I promise."

Philip relaxed. He knew he was probably paranoid, but after what had happened to him, he needed to know Myron would be okay. Technically, his parents or Oscar's family should have Myron if Philip died, but Philip hated that idea. He didn't want any of them to have any say in his son's life. They weren't good people. They didn't deserve it. They'd ruin Myron's life if they were allowed to have anything to do with him.

Philip swallowed and forced himself to smile at Joel. "Thank you. I should probably go downstairs now so we can start as soon as Abel arrives. Myron is going to be hungry when he wakes up."

Joel smiled gently. "I know how to take care of a newborn. I've had plenty of time to learn with my nephew. Don't worry. Besides, if I need anything, you'll be downstairs. I'll come to get you, I swear."

"Thank you." Philip did feel better now that he knew Myron wouldn't be left alone.

He went downstairs, surprised when he noticed Abel's car parked outside. He hadn't realized Abel had arrived, but it helped him relax, especially when he found him in the kitchen, putting together some tea. Abel didn't drink tea, but Philip did. "Hello," Philip said.

Abel smiled. "Hey. I wasn't sure if you needed something, so I got this ready for you."

"Thank you."

"It's nothing. And you have nothing to be worried about. You know that."

"I do." He did, but sometimes, his guts were stronger than his brain. It was so easy to believe that something bad was going to happen, especially with Philip's past being what it was.

Philip was surprised at some of the people who were there when he walked into the living room. He'd expected the alphas and the council members, but what were Eddie, Dimitri, and Alex doing there?

Abel leaned closer. "They want to make sure you know you're safe," he murmured.

Philip's eyes prickled. He didn't want to cry, especially not at something that touched him so much. They hadn't needed to be there for him, to be support he hadn't known he needed. Abel was there, and it was okay, it was enough, but seeing that other people cared for him like this made Philip feel bewildered, and it probably wasn't the best idea, considering what he was about to do.

The rest of the people in the room fell silent, as if they'd just noticed Philip was there. He didn't have contact with most of them. The only people he regularly saw who didn't live with him were Abel, Eddie, and Joel. Even Thomas, the badger alpha, didn't come often. The fewer people did, the better it would be for the needed secrecy. So it was intimidating to meet all these people. They were alphas and council members, and powerful people had too easily behaved badly with Philip in the past. He needed to trust them, though. It was the only way they'd manage to do some good for the people in the forest.

"We can sit down there on the couch," Abel said. He took Philip's hand and gently pulled him in that direction.

Philip didn't miss the way Abel glared around, even though the people there were his friends. He was silently warning them, and it made Philip's' stomach flutter.

Abel really did love him. Philip had heard the words, and he'd believed them, but it was in moments like these that he could *feel* them. He could see how much he meant to Abel, and it helped him settle down.

He could do this. He wouldn't be able to solve any of the prickle's problems, not by himself, but he could help. He'd tell the people in the room what he knew about the prickle and what he thought should happen, and hopefully, they would take things in hand and make sure they did.

Abel knew he was being ridiculous. Everyone in the room was a friend, and they wouldn't do anything to hurt Philip. That didn't stop him from glaring, though. He wanted everyone to know there would be consequences if anything happened to Philip and that he'd be the one who'd make sure of that.

Thomas was grinning like an idiot, while Morris muttered, "No one's going to touch him, dammit."

Abel glared harder. Yes, he was ridiculous, but Philip didn't want to be there. He didn't want to have to think about the people who had abandoned him and the monsters who'd hurt him again, yet there he was, and all because Abel had asked him to. He was nervous, there was no denying that, but he walked with his head high, even though he was clutching Abel's hand.

They settled on the couch. There was a moment of silence, and Abel could have kissed Morris when instead of giving Philip his attention, he looked at Abel instead. "Do you think that Kari guy killed Grimes?"

Abel didn't have any more answers than he'd had yesterday, but they were giving Philip some time to relax and put his thoughts together. "I have no idea, but I wouldn't be surprised."

"Did he say anything about it when you last saw him?"

"No. We *did* talk about the prickle and how things were going to be difficult to change if Grimes didn't appoint a decent person to take Oscar's place, though."

"That could have given him the idea."

"I don't know him well, but I wouldn't be surprised, not after what he did to Oscar. It feels like he's trying to impress us."

Thomas snorted. "By killing people?"

"I think it's working," Morris said. "I'm definitely impressed. Look, I'm not saying we would have killed Oscar and Grimes. It's not what the council or us alphas are about. But they were dangerous, and the forest is a safer place now that they're gone. We're in this to help the carriers, yes? To make sure they have a decent life and can do what they want. Both Oscar and Grimes stood in the way of that, and I, for one, am glad they're gone. They were assholes. They deserve everything they got, and worse. That's not to say I'd trust this Kari with my family, but maybe it's not a bad thing to have a man who's ready to do whatever it takes to keep people safe on our side."

Morris wasn't wrong. Kari might not be right about killing people, and it couldn't become a habit or an easy way out of tricky situations, but in this case, Kari had probably saved their asses. There wouldn't have been any other way to push Oscar and Grimes to the side, even with what they'd done.

It would have been Philip's word against theirs, and Philip wouldn't have been able to speak up anyway because he'd have been taken away. No, this had been the only way, no matter how much Abel regretted it. As long as Kari didn't decide to kill everyone who stood in the way of what they were trying to do, things would be fine. They could finally move ahead now.

Abel cleared his throat. "I don't know if Kari had anything to do with this, but we can ask him when we see him. That's not why we're here today, though. I asked Philip to talk to us about the prickle. As you all know by now, he's a porcupine shifter, and he lived there his entire life. He was isolated for part of it because of Oscar and Grimes, but he knows the people there, including the beta, and he thinks he knows who would be a good alpha."

"And an alpha on our side?" Calder asked.

"That's what we need, as we all know. With the porcupine alpha on our side, the prickle can nominate a council member that will see things the way we do, like Karen."

"Who did you have in mind, then, Philip?" Calder asked.

Philip straightened his back. "Alpha Grimes' oldest daughter."

To the credit of everyone there, they didn't look shocked. Maybe it really was time for things to change in the forest. If a lot of people thought that having a female alpha was acceptable, it meant that the old traditions were starting to fade. That was a good thing.

"He only had daughters, then?" Morris asked. "Or is there a son who will try to stop this?"

Philip relaxed. "Only daughters, three of them. They're all married. I think Lindsay would be the best alpha, and the fact that she's the oldest works in her favor. Of course, the fact that she's a woman doesn't."

"We can probably deal with that."

"The elders will never allow her to take her father's place."

"What about the beta?"

Philip sighed. He was playing with Abel's fingers, carefully not looking at the people around him. "He's not going to be happy. He's been eying the alpha position forever, what with Alpha Grimes not having sons. I think that if you want things to be smoother with the elders, that maybe you could select Lindsay's husband. He's a porcupine shifter, and they have a son, so sooner or later, the alpha position would go back to Alpha Grimes' bloodline. That might keep the elders quiet. There's been a Grimes in charge for the past eighty years, and they want that to continue. Alpha Grimes was an only child, at least from his father's marriage, so there will be no brothers to contend that. Just Beta Robertson. But if you play the husband card, the elders might overrule him."

"What do you think, Philip? Never mind the traditions and the rules. Who do you think should be the next alpha?"

Philip looked up. "Lindsay. I don't know her husband well, but he's always been submissive to Alpha Grimes. That might only be because he was hoping Alpha Grimes would pick him as his heir, but either way, I don't think he'd be a good alpha."

"But Lindsay would."

"She didn't choose her husband. Her father did it for her. But she is a good woman and does what she can for the prickle. I can't imagine it's easy, or that it was easy, with her father being who he was and how he was. I heard them fight plenty of times over a wide array of topics, all related to the health of the prickle. She will be a good alpha if you manage to put her in the position."

Philip sounded convinced, and Abel trusted his opinion. He leaned forward to get everyone's attention. "We all know it's going to be hard to get the prickle to accept that, especially the elders, as Philip pointed out. We could try to get her husband in the role, but that doesn't sound like a good idea. We have to decide if we're going to go down the easiest route, or if we're here to try to change things."

"I don't have anything against changing things," Jerome,

the fox alpha, said. "But like you said, it would be easier if we went with the husband. He might not be the best choice, but we can hope his wife will help guide him."

"But we can send a powerful message here. We can show the rest of the forest that we don't care what's in someone's pants. If they're the right person for the job, then they get it. And there *shouldn't* be a difference between men and woman, or men and carriers. Dan, you want Chris to become the clowder's alpha once you step down. You have to see how important this is to obtain that." Abel was playing dirty, but the time to be nice was over. This was their chance, and they had to take it.

Dan sighed. "You're right. It's not going to be easy, but my vote is for Lindsay. I just hope we can manage that."

"But if we do, she'll be on our side." Hopefully. Abel hadn't yet talked to her, so maybe all of this was a moot point. He didn't think so, though. If Lindsay wanted the best for the prickle, she'd work with them. Besides, Abel trusted Philip's instinct. If he thought Lindsay was the best choice, then it was the one they needed to make.

Philip could tell some of the people in the room didn't like what he was saying. His first instinct was to explain he'd changed his mind and that Lindsay's husband would be good as an alpha, but instead, he squeezed Abel's hand and raised his chin. They'd asked for his opinion, and he'd given it to them. What they did with it was something Philip wouldn't have a say in, but he'd done his part.

The prickle needed a good alpha. Alpha Grimes and his father before him hadn't been good alphas. Philip only vaguely remembered Alpha Grimes' father, but he knew from listening to people talking that while he hadn't been cruel like his son, he'd had a weak spine. He'd let his son push him around as soon as Alpha Grimes had realized he could. And when Alpha Grimes had taken his father's place, he'd started ruining lives.

It was going to take some work for the prickle to get better. They needed to work through the years of abuse they hadn't stood up against. Philip was glad he didn't live there anymore, and the thought that he could be forced to go back if anyone ever found out he was here and unmarried was terrifying.

That didn't mean he didn't want the prickle to heal, though. Maybe in a few years, when Myron was older, Philip would be able to take him there to see where he came from. As much as Philip hated the people who'd hurt him and the ones who hadn't done anything to help him, prickle territory was still the place where he'd grown up. Myron was a porcupine shifter like him. He had a right to go there.

And that wouldn't happen if the prickle didn't have a good alpha. Philip had no idea how Lindsay had managed to grow up into a decent woman, but she had, and she was the prickle's only chance. She could help it heal, but only if they gave her a chance to do so and to prove herself.

"I doubt her husband will be chosen," he said before he could think more about it.

"What do you mean?" Thomas asked.

"Well, it might sound like a good idea." Or decent at the very least. "But Beta Robertson won't allow it, and he has the elders on his side."

"The same can be said for Lindsay. Both she and her husband have something going against them. She's a woman, and he's not related to Grimes."

"Yes, but like I said, the elders want the alpha position to stay in the Grimes family. Lindsay's husband isn't a Grimes, so that goes against their idea. Lindsay never changed her name, though, and she is her father's daughter. Besides, I doubt the elders will be entirely happy with anyone, but the rest of the prickle won't mind Lindsay. They know both her and her husband, and if they want what's best for themselves and their family, they'll know who the best alpha will be."

Morris cleared his throat. "I feel like we could talk about this around and around for hours without getting to a definite solution. It's obvious that both Lindsay and her husband present some problems, but you said Lindsay would be better. Do you still stand by that?"

"I do."

Morris looked around the room. "I say we vote, then. This way, we'll get to a solution right away. Who thinks we should pick Lindsay's husband as the next alpha?"

A few hands shot up, but Philip was relieved to see it wasn't more than a few. And when Morris asked who was in favor of Lindsay, he didn't even have to count to know who they would be supporting.

"Lindsay it is," Morris confirmed. "Now, how do we do this? I doubt she'll be happy with us barging into prickle territory to talk to her."

Philip relaxed against Abel's side. He'd done his job. He could stop thinking about the prickle and focus on his future with Myron and Abel—as far from the prickle as possible.

"I think Philip should talk to her," someone said.

Philip froze. He'd heard that right, he knew it, and it felt as if his throat was closing. The thought of going back to the place where he'd been so unhappy was petrifying, and he might have bolted if Abel hadn't been supporting him.

"What the fuck?" Abel snapped. He never swore, and that told Philip how angry he was right now. "Why would you want Philip to go back to that place? You know what he went through there, and you know what will happen if he goes and someone realizes what happened with Oscar. And how does he explain suddenly returning? Who knows what Grimes told the rest of the prickle?"

Morris raised his hands. Philip couldn't believe he'd been the one to suggest this, then again, he could. Morris wanted the best for everyone in the forest, and that meant getting Lindsay to accept the alpha position. They couldn't exactly send a stranger into prickle territory. They wouldn't be allowed in, and if they managed to sneak in, they'd be shot on sight.

But Philip was a porcupine shifter. The prickle was his home, no matter how much he hated it.

"I'm sorry this sounds harsh," Morris explained. "But I think it's the best way to get Lindsay on board. She knows Philip, and from what Philip told us, she'll probably either already know what was done to him, or she'll believe him when he tells her. She'll see how important this is for everyone. And of course, Philip isn't threatening. He's not another alpha or a council member. He's just someone who's worried about the prickle."

"I'm not saying you're wrong, but that doesn't mean this is what we should do," Abel insisted.

Philip knew he'd stand for him forever, that he'd push back unless Philip himself decided to do this.

He didn't want to. He didn't want to go back to prickle territory so soon after being rescued from it. He didn't want to risk being taken away by the council members who were still on Oscar's side even though he was dead, or to be locked away by the elders because they wanted to auction him.

"We won't send him alone, of course. I'm sure Dimitri, Alex, and a lot of other people will volunteer to go with him and make sure no one hurts him or even thinks about hurting him. But we need to get this right. And having gone through what he's gone through, I feel he's the best ambassador for us. He can explain everything to Lindsay and make her see this is the best outcome for everyone, including the prickle. He can tell her exactly who is going to be against it. He *knows* the prickle and Lindsay, and we don't. Besides, if someone from the council tried to do this, the prickle would no doubt close ranks. The elders would appoint someone just to be sure the council doesn't have a say in it, and they'd pick the wrong person, as we know. We can't risk that, and I'm not just thinking about how we need a porcupine council member who's on our side. I might not be a porcupine, but that doesn't mean I want the prickle to suffer through another who knows how many years of bad leadership and abuse."

"But no matter how many people go with him, it would still be against the law to defend him if some of the council members decide to intervene. No matter how little I like the carrier law, it's still a law, and anyone who tries to stop the council from enforcing it would be in trouble. I doubt you want to risk Dimitri this way, and *I* don't want to risk Philip."

"Philip and Abel should get married."

Philip didn't recognize the voice, and he wasn't the only one. Almost all of them were looking around, trying to identify it. Abel wasn't, though. He was staring at the back of the room, where a short man with brown hair was leaning against the wall, looking bored. Philip knew he didn't belong there with them, that he was neither an alpha nor a council member, but that didn't help.

Then Abel said, "Kari. How did you get in here?" and all hell broke loose.

CHAPTER TEN

The living room was a flurry of movement. Almost everyone shot to their feet. A few people moved toward Kari, but no one seemed to know what to do. He wasn't an enemy, but he also wasn't a friend, not yet.

"Sit down," Abel said. Nothing happened. He was going to need to yell, wasn't he? He sighed, cleared his throat, and tried again. "Sit down, people!"

That got him a bit more attention. "It's Kari," he explained.

The people closest to him had heard, and they passed on the news to the others. Abel glared at Kari, who seemed to find all of this amusing. It probably was, from his point of view. "How did you get in here?" Abel asked him.

Kari shrugged. "I'm not gonna tell you that. Can't give you all my secrets when I still don't know if you're going to give me the job I want or if you're going to have me arrested."

Abel rolled his eyes. He hadn't realized Kari was so dramatic the few times they'd talked. "We're not going to have you arrested."

"Probably," Thomas muttered.

Kari's presence there had to sting for him, and Abel suspected he'd spend at least a half hour after the meeting yelling at the guards who should have made sure no one could enter the Bishop house. If Abel was honest, he wasn't too happy about Kari's presence either. He didn't think the man wanted to hurt any of the carriers, but he didn't know him

133

well enough to be sure of that, and both the man he loved and their son were in the building. Thinking that Kari and possibly anyone else who knew how he managed to sneak in could do it whenever they wanted to made Abel want to grab Philip and Myron and drag them to herd territory. Not that it would be much safer, considering the deer weren't fighters, not even the guards, but it still felt safer, even though it wasn't.

"Did you kill Grimes?" Morris asked.

Kari smiled. "Yep. You liked it?"

Abel groaned. God, Kari was behaving as if killing someone were perfectly reasonable. This wasn't going to endear him with the people in the room, and if he wanted to be a part of the team they were putting together, he needed them to like him. "Can we all sit down for a moment?" he asked, hoping to defuse the situation. He knew he was going to have to face this line of questioning anyway, but he hoped to be able to do it without people yelling at each other.

When had Abel become their group's unofficial spokesman anyway? He hated being at the center of attention, yet there he was, right in the middle of things.

He waited until everyone was back in their seat, except Kari, who was still leaning against the wall. Abel sighed. He didn't want to do this, dammit. "I'm not going to ask how you got in here since you won't answer, but you have to realize why everyone here is wary of you," he told Kari.

Kari's shoulders lowered. "I'm not going to hurt anyone here."

"We only have your word for that," Thomas said. Abel glared at him, but they weren't in school, and he couldn't very well put Thomas in the corner for voicing his opinion.

"I guess we're going to have to trust each other. I mean, I have no doubt you could grab me right now and lock me up, and I wouldn't be able to do much against it. There's only one of me and a lot of you. No matter how good I am at defending myself, I couldn't do much."

Thomas grumbled, but he didn't add anything, and Abel was grateful for that. "Now that that's clarified, what are you doing here, Kari?"

"Well, since you managed to get your people together sooner than expected . . ."

"Not everyone is here, and all of us have a say in pulling you into the team. You won't get an answer tonight."

"That's fine. I also wanted to see what you were going to do about the whole Grimes thing. You know, since he's dead."

"How did you do it? We were told it was a heart attack." And they still hadn't heard anything different. Although Abel wasn't surprised to find out Kari had something to do with it.

"You know, there are a lot of plants in the forest that can cause death. I also know people who can procure me whatever I ask for."

"So you poisoned him."

Kari grinned. "And I watched him die to be sure he was done for. There's no need to thank me, though. I did it for everyone in the forest. Our lives will be nicer without that asshole in it."

"You know, we might not need that team anymore," Morris said. He was staring at Kari. "I mean, if we manage to get Grimes' daughter in his position and on our side, she'll pick a council member we can deal with, and we'll be able to officially send people in the territories to check on the carriers."

Kari snorted. "Because they're going to let you in. Please. I mean, I get what you're saying, and I even think it wouldn't be a bad thing, but that's not what the council is about, and you know it, no doubt better than me. You guys are supposed to make sure all the shifters in the forest are at peace with each other, or at least that they don't kill each other. That doesn't give you the authority to go into their territories, especially with no proof that they'd abusing their carriers, or anyone else for that matter. No, you need the team, although it would be better if it weren't associated with the council. And I want to be in it."

That made sense, but Abel could see no one wanted to admit it. Kari wasn't wrong, though. The council had been created to keep the peace between the shifter groups who lived in the forest, not to police the way the alphas behaved. People would revolt if the council's reach widened, but they wouldn't be able to say anything if someone they didn't know snuck into their territory and took the people they were abusing away. Of course, they'd then have to find a way to replace the bad alphas and make sure something like that never happened again, but it would be a huge first step, and it was one they needed to make. Abel could too easily imagine how much the carriers were suffering at this moment. Philip had gone through it, and Abel didn't want anyone else ever to have to again.

Thomas huffed. "Fine. You have my vote."

Abel's eyes widened. He'd thought Thomas would need a lot of convincing, especially since Kari had broken into the Bishop house even with the guards, the alphas, and the council members being there.

Thomas seemed to realize he'd stunned everyone. "What? I can admit when I'm wrong. I might not like Kari one bit, but that doesn't change the fact that he had more than one opportunity to hurt anyone in this house, including my sons and me. He hasn't. I don't trust him fully, but I do believe him when he says he's in this for the same reason we are and that he's not going to turn against us."

Kari beamed. "That's settled, then."

"Not yet," Abel reminded him, but they all knew the others would probably follow suit. "But you have my vote, too."

The people sitting in the living room all nodded, one by one. Some of them didn't look convinced, and Abel didn't blame them. Still, they realized they needed Kari.

"So, now that this is cleared up, what did you mean when you said that Philip and Abel should get married?" Morris asked.

Philip tensed next to Abel. Abel would have paid to know what he was thinking. He'd heard Kari's words, of course, but he hadn't had the time to think about them. He doubted Philip had, either.

Philip had heard Kari the first time he'd said that, of course. He hadn't reacted to it because so much had been going on, and it had been easy to focus on everything else. Then Morris had asked Kari what he'd meant, and now Philip was going to have to face his answer.

He wasn't sure he wanted to know.

Oh, he wished he and Abel could get married. He'd say yes in a heartbeat if he thought Abel wanted it as much as he did. Hell, he'd ask Abel if he thought Abel would say yes. He didn't, though.

They were together, but it was so new. Philip didn't think Abel would change his mind about them, but he didn't want to shake things up, just in case. Abel already had enough to worry about.

"Well, I thought it was obvious," Kari asked. He sounded like he thought they were all idiots, and he probably wasn't wrong. Philip certainly felt like an idiot right now, with people talking about him and his relationship as if he weren't even in the room.

"Maybe it is. I'd like to hear it from you, though."

"All right. You're thinking about sending Philip to the prickle to talk to Grimes' daughter. You can't do it, though, because they could report his presence to the council, and you'd have to have him taken away, as the law says right now. But if he were married, no one would be able to do that, especially if he was there with his husband."

"I can't go," Abel said. "I'm a council member."

"You wouldn't be there in that capacity, though. You'd be there as Philip's husband, and no one can say anything about that. It's in everyone's best interest, since Philip technically has a say in who the next alpha will be."

Philip snapped his head up. "What are you talking about?" He didn't bother trying to hide the surprise or the wariness in his voice. Everyone knew how he felt anyway. It was no doubt evident on his face.

"You gave birth to Oscar's son, right?"

Philip swallowed. "I did." He might not like that thought, but he couldn't deny it.

"Myron is *my* son," Abel said.

A few eyebrows in the room shot up at his declaration. Philip leaned closer to him, though. Hearing him claiming Myron so publicly was a balm on his battered soul. It wasn't only a private promise anymore.

Kari waved Abel's words away. "I get that, but that's not what I was talking about. Willing or not, Philip did give birth to Oscar's son, and I have no doubt that the prickle knew about it. I can't imagine Oscar wouldn't have boasted about getting a carrier pregnant, and since Philip was the prickle's only carrier, it doesn't take a genius to know who the other father was. What I'm saying is that Oscar would have had a say in who the next alpha will be if he'd been alive, because of his position in the prickle. Since he's gone, that honor, or however you want to call it, goes to his son. Myron is too young, though. That means his *father* can make this kind of decision for him. Philip."

Philip's stomach churned. He'd never had that kind of power. He didn't *want* that kind of power, and he didn't want to go back to the prickle and face the people who hadn't done anything to help him.

Because Kari was right—everyone in the prickle knew he was a carrier. It had become public knowledge as soon as the healer had realized. She'd told Alpha Grimes, and the news had spread from there. And when Philip had been taken from his home by Oscar, everyone had known about it. They'd known *why* Oscar was taking Philip away, and none of them had protested. They hadn't tried to stop what was happening.

Philip didn't doubt that Oscar had told people he was expecting his son. He'd have had to. He couldn't just appear one day with a baby and not give at least some kind of explanation. So the prickle members knew Philip was Myron's father. They might try to act as if they couldn't know whether Myron was effectively Oscar's son, but everyone would know they were full of shit.

So Philip *did* have a say in the next alpha. He'd thought he'd only be able to give Lindsay a push, but maybe he could do more than that. He could give her a fighting chance against the elders. He wasn't the one who'd made the rules that the other parent of a council member—or even an alpha's—could speak for their dead partner or their children. The elders wouldn't be able to work around that because *they'd* been the one to come up with it.

But Philip couldn't go to the prickle if he wasn't married. It would be too dangerous, and the elders would use that against him, to make sure he couldn't speak in Oscar's place for Lindsay.

The only person he wanted to marry was Abel, of course, but did Abel want the same thing?

"We can't force them to get married just because Philip needs protection," Thomas said.

"Oh, please. We wouldn't be forcing them. They've been making puppy eyes at each other since they met, and you heard Abel. Myron is his son. That has to mean something," Kari said.

God, Philip hated this. He didn't want him and Abel to be pushed into something they weren't ready for, but it did sound like the only way to get what they needed without hurting anyone.

"None of that matters. Unless they both agree they're ready to do this, no one here is going to push them for it. We'll find another way to influence the elders and get Lindsay into the alpha position."

Philip thought they might be able to do it, but what would it cost them? How long would it take? They didn't have much time. The elders knew what was at stake here, and they'd make sure no one but them could take advantage of the situation. Philip wasn't sure why they hadn't named anyone yet, but they were going to, and fast.

Philip had to go to the prickle. He had to talk to Lindsay and make sure she became the alpha.

And to do that, he had to be married.

Kari disappeared. Abel wasn't sure how or when he'd managed to slip out, but when the rest of them had stopped arguing back and forth about Philip and Abel getting married, he was gone. Abel hadn't been surprised, not with what he knew of Kari. He also knew Kari would be back, probably after they solved this problem with the prickle.

He wasn't looking forward to it.

He didn't hate Kari, but he wasn't happy with him. Kari shouldn't have brought up the wedding thing, even though it was probably the only solution they could use. They didn't have enough time to try to influence the prickle and the elders, but having Philip weigh in as Myron's father would do that. And the only way for Philip to be safe when he went to the prickle was for him to be married.

Being married to a council member would give him all the protection he'd need. Abel doubted the elders would try anything, but the beta might. Attacking a council member and his husband would be unforgivable, and he'd lose the alpha position. But if he went along with things, he might be able to stay as the beta. Abel hoped not, with what he knew about the man, but that wasn't something he would have to deal with.

But of course, the logic behind him and Philip getting married wasn't what Abel was obsessing over. No, he couldn't help thinking about what Philip would look like next to him at the altar, about what his voice would sound like as he said his vows.

Was that something Philip might want? Abel wished it hadn't been brought up in this situation this soon after he and Philip had gotten together, but there was no changing that.

He'd been avoiding looking at Philip since Kari had brought this up, just in case. He wasn't sure what he'd do if he saw rejection on Philip's face. Not that he wouldn't understand it, but that didn't mean he wanted to see it.

"Abel?"

Abel looked at Calder. He'd gotten up to say goodbye to the first people leaving. It had put some distance between him and Philip, who was quietly talking with Eddie and Alex, their heads close together. Were they talking about Abel and the marriage possibility?

"Abel? Are you okay?"

Right. Abel had already forgotten about Calder. "I'm fine," he said, turning his attention back to his friend.

"Are you sure? Because you don't look fine. That guy dropped a lot on you, huh?"

"I can't say I ever expected my wedding to be the talk of one of our meetings, no."

Calder didn't smile. "I wouldn't have, either. You don't have to do it just because you think it's the best thing to do."

"It is, though."

"Maybe, but for whom? Not for you and Philip, unless you both want it. We can find another way to get through to the elders. I'm not above threatening them to stick their asses in jail because of what they allowed to happen. There might not be a specific law that forbids the abuse of carriers, but that doesn't mean they should, and if they try to argue that carriers aren't normal shifters, I'll kick their ass myself."

Abel smiled. He'd known he'd have his friends' support, but hearing it made him feel better. He hoped the same was going on with Philip. He didn't want them to fight, especially not over this. "I know we don't have to do it."

"Yet you feel the responsibility to."

"Partly. I also just really want to marry Philip, though."

Calder's eyes widened. "Dammit. I hate that we haven't had the time to keep up with each other. I mean, I knew you were in love with him and everything, although I doubt anyone *wasn't* aware of that, but I didn't realize it was so deep on your part."

"I told Kari I was Myron's dad."

"Yeah, but I thought you were trying to protect Philip. That's kind of your thing. So you love him?"

"Very much so." Abel couldn't help but look back at Philip. His heart always felt so full when he looked at the man he loved and when they spent time together. It was a nice sensation, albeit a bit unusual for Abel to feel.

"And I suspect he loves you, too."

"He does." Abel wasn't going to doubt Philip's word on that. They were past that, and he was never going back.

"So you two might not be against this marriage?"

Abel sighed. "I'll be honest—I *was* planning on asking him sooner or later."

"But not like this."

"And not now. I didn't want him to feel like he had to say yes, you know? Right now, he's stuck here. He can't leave because he could get caught. I don't want him to say yes just because he needs to be free."

"I doubt he'd do that."

Abel smiled. "I don't think he would, either. It's my fears speaking out. But we haven't been together long, and we've never lived together. We're still trying to fit into each other's life."

"And I bet that's not easy, considering what's happening and how you both have to live."

"You're right, it's not."

Calder peered at Abel. "You're going to do it, aren't you?"

Abel tried to look innocent, but he and Calder had been working together for years, and they'd been friends just as long. Calder knew how to read him. "Do what?"

Calder leaned closer. "Propose. Do you even have a ring?"

"No, but I'm sure I can find something."

"So you *are* going to propose?"

"Yes." Abel hadn't been able to stop thinking about it since Kari had mentioned it. He knew it was too soon, that Philip might say no, or that he might say yes for the wrong reason, but he also knew they loved each other and that they worked well together. Their future was with each other, and so what if they had to rush into things? They wouldn't be the only ones ever to do it. Hell, most married couples around there had rushed into things. Being a carrier made Philip vulnerable, even though it shouldn't. This was a way to keep him safe.

Calder patted Abel's shoulder. "Well, let me know when he says yes. I know we can't do much of a party considering the circumstances, but I'm sure we'll manage something."

"You don't have to do that."

"Maybe not, but I want to, and I know I won't be the only one."

The rest of the alphas and council members filtered away until only the people who lived there were left in the living room—and Abel. Chris had come in at some point and was spread on the couch watching TV, but Abel ignored him. "Philip?"

Philip turned to look at him with wide eyes. "Yes?"

"Do you think Joel will be fine with keeping an eye on Myron for another little while?"

"I think so, yes. Why?" He licked his lips. "Do you want to talk?"

"I thought we could shift and have a run in the forest. I know you haven't had many opportunities to do that lately, between Myron and the safety measures. Want to take advantage now?"

Philip nodded. Abel realized he was postponing the inevitable conversation they'd have to have, but that was okay. They could take half an hour to relax and stop thinking about everything. The problems weren't going anywhere anyway.

They went outside. Abel could tell Philip was nervous, but he ignored it. He took Philip's hand and kissed him, smiled at him and said, "We'll talk later, okay?"

Philip nodded. "I just . . ."

"I know. We can have fun for a little while. Come on. Shift."

Abel turned around to give Philip some privacy. He hadn't missed the way Philip hadn't gotten naked with him yet, and he didn't want to make him uncomfortable. He turned back only when something pulled at his pants.

He looked down, grinning. "I can't say I've seen a lot of porcupine shifters in my life, but you're pretty." Although maybe pretty wasn't the best word. Philip looked fierce, with all the spikes shooting from his body. His face was cute, though, especially when he wiggled his nose like he was doing now.

"Go on. I'll be right there," Because while Abel *had* been naked with Philip, he wasn't entirely comfortable with it yet.

He watched Philip waddle away. He was going to marry that man, either now or later, once this mess was over. Abel wanted it, and he suspected Philip did, too.

He just had to find out if he was right about that.

CHAPTER ELEVEN

Philip was glad he and Abel were in their animal forms. That way, he didn't have to talk. He wasn't sure what he would have said if he could have, but he couldn't stop thinking about Kari's suggestion that they get married.

He didn't think he would forget about it until he and Abel talked and Abel confirmed he didn't want that.

Because Phillip did, so very much.

It was probably ridiculous to think about marrying a man he hadn't known long, even though Philip had known that was what would happen to him. He'd expected Alpha Grimes to choose someone for him when he was younger, someone that would give something to the prickle in exchange. Then, when Oscar had taken him away, he'd thought he'd never get married. He hadn't been able to imagine a life outside the cell Oscar had put him in.

And then Alex and his friends had rescued him.

Philip had been free for six months now, and he'd known Abel for just as long. He'd known he loved Abel since the beginning, and from what Abel had told him, so had he. So was it too soon to think about getting married? They hadn't been a couple long, but that didn't change the fact that they'd been friends before becoming one.

But all of Philip's obsessing over this wouldn't help him, not when he couldn't even ask Abel what he was thinking. Maybe that was why Abel had wanted to shift. Maybe he didn't want to talk about this, and it was easier to brush Philip off this way. Philip could ask, of course, but he didn't want to rock their relationship. He didn't want to risk it.

So he decided to not ask about it, not even once they shifted back to their human form. That might make him a coward, but he didn't think his heart could take a rejection this big. It was still healing, still trying to become whole, and Abel was helping a lot with that. Philip didn't want things to be awkward between them, and he didn't want Abel to feel obligated or to give him an explanation that would hurt both of them.

He looked up, trying to find Abel. It had been a while since he'd shifted — Abel hadn't been wrong when he'd said that Myron took a lot of energy out of Philip — and it had felt like slipping back into his skin. Life as a porcupine was infinitely easier than it was as a human, even though Philip couldn't stop thinking about Abel and marrying him. That was *all* he thought about, though, so it was more relaxing.

Abel was bouncing somewhere in front of Philip. Philip had tried to keep up in the beginning, but it was so much nicer to stay on his ass and watch Abel have fun. And he certainly looked like he was having fun. Philip didn't think he'd ever seen a deer behaving this way, although of course, Abel wasn't just a deer. There was a human mind in him, and that was the thing that made it fun.

Philip couldn't see much more than movement since it was dark, but he'd gotten a good look at Abel earlier when they'd shifted by the house. His deer coat was warm brown, and it made Philip wonder if it was as soft as it looked. God knew Abel would never pet *him* in his animal form. It was possible, but no one had ever offered. Philip knew he was slightly intimidating, with all the needles sticking out of his body, and that was okay. He wasn't sure he'd want people randomly touching him because he looked cute. He could imagine petting Abel, though, both in his animal form *and* in his human form.

That thought startled Philip. He and Abel hadn't had the opportunity to spend another night together, and Philip had been thinking about the one they'd had almost obsessively. Walking up with Abel in his bed had been delightful, but Philip's thoughts also often went back to the evening before that.

He'd had sex, and it hadn't hurt. That made him want to do it again, and he wasn't sure how to deal with it. He'd never been in this kind of situation, and everything else happening around them wasn't helping him to think about it rationally.

He sighed. Maybe he should give Abel some time on his own. He was having fun, while Philip couldn't stop thinking long enough to feel that way. He should go back to Myron and make his evening at least in part productive. Abel would know he'd be inside, and maybe they could talk, but Philip wasn't going to push. They probably both needed some time to wrap their minds around what was going to happen and what would need to be done because of it.

He raised his butt and walked toward the house. He didn't think Abel had noticed him in a while, so he shifted before he got to the back door. He and Abel had left their clothes there, so he wouldn't have to go inside naked. He winced when he set his foot on a big pebble. Maybe he should have stayed in his porcupine form a bit longer.

He was dressed and reaching for the door when he could tell Abel spotted him. He'd tried to be quick and silent—he had some training with that since he often woke up before Myron in the morning—but he still lacked in that department.

Abel bounded toward him, and Philip rubbed the back of his neck. "I'm just going inside to check on Myron. You can stay out here, though. Have some more fun. I'll see you later, or tomorrow if you need to go home."

Philip grabbed the door handle, but Abel didn't give him time to flee. "Philip."

Abel was naked. Of course he was. He'd just shifted. Philip kept his gaze fixed on Abel's face because he knew Abel wasn't comfortable being naked. "Yes?"

"Don't you think we need to talk?"

"Of course, but it can wait tomorrow." That would be soon enough to face this. Too soon, actually.

"I don't think it can." Abel stepped forward, looked down, and swore. "Dammit. Can you give me a second to get dressed? I don't want to talk to you while I'm naked."

"Of course."

"I meant, please stay here?"

Philip had been planning to wait inside so he could maybe gather his thoughts, but of course, Abel would want some privacy.

Philip let go of the handle and leaned against the side of the house. He made sure he didn't look in Abel's direction, no matter how much he wanted to. He liked Abel's body and how safe it had made him feel that night.

"All right. What's wrong, Philip?" Abel asked.

When Philip looked at him, he saw that Abel was still buttoning his shirt. His feet were bare, but he didn't seem to care.

"Nothing's wrong. Well, nothing more than what's already been wrong for a while."

Abel narrowed his eyes. "There's more to it. I can tell. I thought we could have fun shifting, but you didn't seem to be happy about it."

"It's not that." Philip was going to have to ask sooner or later. He supposed he might as well do it now, rip off the plaster or whatever. "What Kari said."

Abel blinked. "What did he say?"

"About the wedding. Yours and mine."

Abel's expression fell. "Of course. Look, we don't have to do this. I understand it's too soon for you and that while you love me, I'm not what you had in mind when you thought of marriage. I'm not going to leave just because you don't want that. It's okay. I would never force you into anything, and that includes marriage, even if it's for the reasons we know are at play here. I hope you know that."

Philip wasn't sure he'd understood Abel's words in the right sense. "What?"

Abel shrugged. He wasn't looking at Philip, and Philip desperately wanted him to. He *needed* to know what was going on. "I said that I understand I'm not exactly a dream husband. It's okay. I won't break up with you because you don't want to marry me. You don't need to worry about this. We'll find another way to deal with prickle."

What the fuck was Abel talking about?

Abel had known this was coming, but he'd hoped they would have a little more time before they had to face it. He'd known they wouldn't, though. The marriage was too important to ignore the situation.

"What are you talking about?" Philip asked.

Hadn't Abel been clear? "About the wedding. I know what Kari said made sense, but that doesn't mean we have to do it. I understand you're not in the right place—"

"That. *That's* what I wanted to know. Do you really think I don't want to marry you?"

Abel hoped those words meant what he thought they meant. "You didn't look ecstatic about it."

"Neither did you, Abel. And let's admit it, this isn't the best way things could go. We haven't been together long, and we don't even live together. And of course, that's not even considering what's happening outside cete territory. I also hate that we're being pushed into this, even though the reasons are good ones. None of that means I don't *want* to do it, though."

That was the most Abel had heard Philip talk, and he'd never sounded so passionate. "I just assumed . . . ."

Philip smiled. "I know. And I assumed the same thing, that you didn't want to marry me, that maybe you weren't ready or that you didn't want to shackle yourself to me."

"Shackle? Philip, I love you. I couldn't be happier than if you married me."

Philip stepped closer. "The same goes for me. I love you, Abel. This might not be the proposal I used to dream of as a kid or the circumstances I would have picked if I could have, but it doesn't change the fact that I love you and that I want to spend the rest of my life with you."

"Ask him properly!" someone yelled from inside the house.

Abel laughed when he saw half the people in the house had gathered around the windows to stare at them. Thank God this was going well, or he'd be utterly humiliated.

Philip's cheeks were flushed, and he looked like he didn't know what to do. Abel needed to take things in hand, and that was okay with him. He didn't have a ring, but that didn't mean he couldn't propose, so he dropped to one knee, not caring that his pants would get dirty.

Philip's eyes went wide. Abel took his hand and squeezed it. This was it. This was the moment Abel would never have thought would happen, especially not with Philip. But it settled something in Abel. He knew what Philip would say now, and it made it easy — but no less exciting — to say the words. "Philip. I love you. I've loved you since the first time I saw you. You were terrified, but you trusted me enough to let me help you into the house, and that will stay with me forever. I hope *you* will stay with me forever. So, Philip. Will you marry me and make me the happiest man on earth?" Okay, so maybe Abel was particularly cheesy, but he'd only get to propose once.

Philip laughed. "Yes. Of course I will."

The whoops and shouts from inside barely filtered through Abel's brain. He was too focused on Philip, who was pulling him up and into his arms, hugging him, crying and laughing at the same time. Abel cupped his cheeks with both hands and kissed him. It was a bit desperate but so good, and now, Abel would be able to do it for the rest of his life.

"Holy shit. We're engaged," he murmured.

Philip's eyes glittered. "I hope you realized that this was what proposing to me would mean before you did it."

"Yeah. I've wanted you to be my husband for weeks, Philip. I hate that—"

Philip shook his head. "Why we're doing it doesn't matter, except because we love each other. There's no need for us to wait. We know what we want."

"You're so good for me."

"I don't know about that, but you definitely are good for me."

"Stop making out and come celebrate!" Chris yelled from the back door.

Abel laughed again. He wasn't sure he'd ever stop. How could he, when he felt this happy? But when he looked up, Chris was holding Myron, and Abel wanted to include the baby in their celebration. He wouldn't understand, but Philip and Abel would, and they'd be able to tell him when he was older.

And apparently, show him pictures, because when Abel and Philip stepped into the kitchen, there were at least six phones turned their way, snapping and recording. Abel hated having pictures taken of him, but he didn't say anything.

This was one of the happiest moments in his life, and for once, he wanted memories of it, memories he could look at and show Myron once he was older.

"We don't have champagne, but I found some orange juice in the fridge," Joel said. He'd already gathered glasses, and he started filling them with the juice.

Abel was a bit lost, but he clung to Philip.

He hadn't realized people would be so happy for them. He knew they cared for both of them, even loved Philip, but he realized that for them, this wedding was vital because it would make sure the forest was safe and that the carriers would be able to go back to their lives.

But they *did* care. Everyone was there now, even Calum, and he *never* spent any time except for meals out of his bedroom. Yet there he was, sipping at the glass Joel had handed him, looking uncomfortable. But he was there, and that meant something to Philip. That was all Abel cared about.

"So, when is the big day?" Chris asked. He'd given Myron back to Philip, and he was grinning maniacally.

Abel was almost afraid to answer. "I don't know, but soon." Philip needed to go to the prickle as soon as possible. "A matter of days."

Chris whistled. "Damn, you're not taking things slow once you made your decision."

Abel sighed. "I want to marry him, but that's not the only reason we're doing this. That means we need to be fast."

Chris cracked his knuckles. "Leave that to me."

Abel was suddenly afraid. "What do you mean?"

"I'll organize everything. I'll need some help from people who can drive back and forth, but you'll have your wedding. You just need to tell me the exact date."

"The day after tomorrow," Philip said.

Chris grimaced. "That's close. But never mind. I can do it. So, an evening wedding, right? In the backyard, maybe? I don't think enough people could fit in here."

"A small ceremony, Chris. No matter how much we might want to invite people, we can't afford to bring too much attention to this place," Abel warned.

Chris rolled his eyes. "I know that. I live here, remember? It'll be us, Thomas, of course since he'll be marrying you, Eddie and Joel, I think, and that's it."

Abel hated that his sister wouldn't be there, but she'd understand. She wanted to keep her son safe above all, and she'd do anything to obtain that, even skip her brother's wedding. Maybe Abel and Philip could get married again once this was over and have a bigger ceremony, at the very least to include Abel's family and their friends.

"I need a few things from you," Chris said.

"Do what you can. No pink," Abel added because he knew Chris.

"No pink. That's not your color anyway."

Thank God for small mercies. "Thank you, Chris." He didn't have to offer himself to organize this, yet he had. They were friends, yes, but assembling a wedding in two days wasn't going to be an easy feat, especially because Chris couldn't leave the house.

Abel didn't care about it. The ceremony was important, of course, and who was there or not mattered, but everything else didn't. He wanted Philip to have a nice wedding, though, something he could remember with fondness when he thought about it in a few years. If letting Chris take charge did that, then Abel was all for it.

Chris wiggled his fingers at Myron. "Why don't you give me the little tyke and sneak upstairs? I'll make sure no one asks where you two are." He grinned. "I'm pretty sure they'll find out anyway." He wiggled his eyebrows, making the meaning of his words clear.

Philip blushed, and suddenly, Abel wanted nothing more

than to be alone with him in his bedroom.

Philip was nervous even though he and Abel had already done this. Well, not this exactly. He wasn't even sure what they were going to do. Maybe they'd cuddle in bed. He'd be happy with that, or with anything else they might do.

He'd still asked Joel for some lube the day before. There had been much blushing and stammering on his part, and only smiling on Joel's, but now Philip had the lube. That didn't mean he had to use it, but he'd wanted to be prepared.

He'd thought about it. He wasn't sure he'd be comfortable with being naked with Abel, not yet, but he didn't need to be to make love with the man who would become his husband in just a few days. He supposed they should wait until they were married to have sex, but it wasn't like he was a virgin, and he didn't see a reason to wait. They could celebrate twice, or every day for the rest of their lives.

"What did you have in mind?" Abel asked as they walked into the bedroom.

It was weird not to have Myron in his arms or in the crib. That was usually the case when he was in his bedroom. It was probably going to change, though. "What's going to happen once we're married? I can't move in with you. Can I?" Philip wanted to spend every day with Abel, but the forest wasn't safe yet, and he couldn't put Myron in danger, especially not if he was going to poke at the prickle's elders.

Abel sighed. "I know you're already worrying about that, but we can talk about it tomorrow, okay? I'm not going to demand that you move in with the herd if you're not comfortable with that, though. I do want to be with you, to live with you, but these aren't normal times, and we can't just do what someone else might do."

Philip should have known Abel would say that. He was so understanding, and his main objective was to keep Philip and Myron safe.

Philip relaxed. "Chris said he'd keep Myron for the night."

"I know he did, but are you ready to leave him with Chris that long? I know you've never slept away from him since he was born."

Philip hadn't expected it to happen, especially not with Myron being only three months old, and it *was* an odd feeling, but that didn't mean he wasn't looking forward to spending the entire night in Abel's arms sleeping. Was he even going to be able to sleep through the night?

"Why don't we both take a shower to get the dust off and get into bed?" Abel suggested. He probably could see Philip was nervous.

"That's a good idea." Philip walked to the bathroom door. He took a deep breath and looked back. "Why don't we share the shower?"

Abel blinked. "Share? As in . . ."

"As in, we can shower together. If that's okay with you." Philip realized he was going to have to be naked to do that, but he hoped that being in a mostly non-sexual situation would help. Of course, they *could* have sex in the shower, but he doubted they would, and not being in bed hopefully would make him feel more comfortable. And Abel, too. Philip knew Abel wasn't comfortable with his body, and he wanted that to change. It wouldn't happen with a shower, but it was a place to start.

"Are you sure? You know I don't expect anything from you."

"I know." That was why Philip was comfortable enough to do this. "You don't expect anything, and I can say stop at any moment even if I already said yes to something before. I trust you, Abel. I wouldn't want to marry you if I didn't. And you can trust me."

"I do."

Philip took Abel's hand and pulled him into the bathroom. He'd wanted things to be sexy, but they were mostly awkward as they stripped in front of each other for the second time that day. They both avoided looking at each other. Philip hated that they weren't comfortable, but it would take time. He was all too aware of that.

Things got better once they were in the shower. There was a moment in which they both hesitated, but then Abel reached for the soap and held it up. "Can I wash you? Only where you feel comfortable."

Philip smiled. "I like it when you touch me, Abel."

"Good. Because I like touching you."

And he did. He lathered his hands and put the soap back. When he reached for Philip, he moved slowly, carefully, stroking his hands over Philip's body. He started with his arms, tickling under Philip's armpits. Philip hadn't even realized he was ticklish until now.

Then Abel moved down to Philip's waist. He avoided Philip's ass, and Philip loved him all the more for it. Still, he wanted to push himself. He wanted to know how far he could get before he started freaking out.

He'd never been in this situation with Oscar. He'd never been in love and loved.

He took Abel's hand and pulled it around himself, pressing it against his ass cheek. Abel was looking at him with understanding and awe in his eyes, and Philip leaned closer to him, kissing him. Everything was better with Abel, even a shower.

Philip shuddered when Abel's fingers slipped between his ass cheeks. They brushed against his hole, and he held his breath, waiting to see if the memories would hit him.

They were there. There was no denying that. Oscar had been the only one who'd touched him there—Arlene didn't count—and Philip couldn't ignore that.

But he could push the memories away. He wrapped himself around Abel, burying his face against Abel's throat. Abel made a soothing sound and started to move his hand, but Philip shook his head. "No. Please."

Abel didn't ask if he was sure, and Philip was glad for that.

He focused on Abel's scent, on how good he felt, how solid and secure. Philip loved him because of who he was, but also because of what he represented. He was the future. He was safety and comfort and love.

They were both hard. Philip rubbed against Abel and clutched his shoulders. He couldn't get closer, but he wanted to. He wanted to be one with Abel.

Not in the shower, though, and probably not today because having Abel touch his ass felt *good*. Philip would never have expected that, but he couldn't deny it, and he wanted more. He wanted Abel inside him, around him. He wanted Abel to make him come.

"We should move to the bedroom," Abel murmured.

"No time."

Philip was sure Abel smiled when he said, "Already there, huh?"

"It's your fault. You feel so good. Everything feels so good."

"Let go, Philip. This is for you. You're reclaiming what was taken from you, as is right."

Philip reached between them, but Abel shook his head. Philip understood what he was saying, but he didn't like it. He wanted Abel to be with him, to feel the same way he did.

He rubbed his hands over Abel's body and pushed closer. He smiled when Abel whined, only to whine himself when the finger that had been rubbing his rim pushed in gently.

There was no pain. It was strange after so long, but Philip recognized the pressure, and he knew what was coming. He focused on Abel, on how his body felt, on how hard he was breathing, on the water that was still coming down on them. It was going to become cold soon, and the thought made Philip chuckle.

"That's not the reaction I'd expected from this position," Abel muttered.

"I'm not laughing at you. I love this, Abel. I love *you*."

They kissed, and there was no more talking after that. Philip never forgot who he was with. He couldn't have even if he'd wanted to. Abel was there, sinking under Philips's skin, touching him and breathing along with him. He wasn't inside of Philip, but they were one nonetheless.

This was what Philip wanted from his future, and he was ready to do anything to get it. He'd face the prickle, and he'd win the fight with them, and with the council if they tried to take him away.

They wouldn't, though. Philip and Abel were getting married, and no one would be able to sever that bond.

CHAPTER TWELVE

A bel couldn't breathe. He was trying, but the sight of Philip looking at him from where he stood between the chairs, about to walk toward him, took his breath away.

"Relax," Thomas whispered from next to Abel.

"I can't."

"I never understood why people are so worried about weddings, especially the ones born of love. He's not going to run away. He loves you. He wants this."

"I know."

"Then what's the problem?"

Abel turned to glare at Thomas. "Really? Can't you remember when you married your wife?"

"Of course I can. I wasn't nervous."

Abel wasn't sure he could believe that, but it didn't matter, because when he looked back at Philip, he was standing in front of him. Myron gurgled and reached for Abel. Abel offered him his hand to play with while wrapping his other arm around Philip's waist.

Thomas chuckled. "He's *not* going to run, Abel."

The small crowd behind them laughed. Abel wasn't even offended. Now that Philip was there next to him, he felt better. He hadn't thought Philip would change his mind, but he was relieved.

Not many people had come. The carriers and most of the guards were there, as was Thomas' family. A few alphas had come, and of course, Calder. That was it, even though Chris had been a genius and had placed a computer on a small table by Abel. It was open, and Abel could see his sisters watching from herd territory. It had been a nice gesture, something Abel wouldn't forget. Chris cared, much more than Abel had initially thought. He was a good friend to Philip, and Philip needed all the friends he could have.

"Ready to begin?" Thomas asked.

Abel was dazed, but he managed to nod.

He'd never thought he'd have this. He'd focused on his work for so long, had ignored the part of him that wanted a relationship, and now he had everything. He wasn't sure what he'd have done if he hadn't met Philip, but he could imagine all too well how dull his life would have been. He'd be alone in his office right now, working.

But instead, he was marrying Philip.

Thomas was talking, and Abel forced himself to connect. He'd already heard this speech, though, and not even that long ago. Thomas needed to start working on his speeches if he was going to celebrate more weddings.

Philip turned toward Abel. Myron was between them, babbling and pulling on Abel's tie. Abel kissed the top of his head, and his heart almost exploded when, prompted by Thomas, Philip said I *do.*

Thomas turned to Abel. "And you, Abel—"

"I do."

Thomas chuckled. "Not even going to listen to what I have to say, are you?"

"I don't need to. I do. I take Philip as my husband, for better and for worse and everything in between, until death do us apart. That's what you were going to say, isn't it?"

Thomas sighed dramatically and waved. "Go ahead, then. I now declare you husband and husband, and of course, you may kiss the groom."

That, he didn't have to repeat. Abel pulled his hand from Myron's grasp and cupped Philip's cheek. He leaned forward, careful of Myron, and kissed his husband until Myron pulled on his tie hard enough to almost strangle him.

That got a laugh out of everyone and broke the spell Abel had been under. Now was the time to celebrate and to be happy. Reality would push its way through soon enough.

Chris had done a great job with the little time he'd had. He and the others had brought a few tables outside, and they'd spread food there. It was enough to feed everyone present and then some. Lanterns had been hung, along with what seemed to be Christmas lights. There was music, and even though there wasn't a dance floor, people were dancing anyway, at least those who weren't eating.

Abel settled Philip into one of the chairs and kissed the top of his head, then Myron's. "I'll be right back. I'm going to get you some food."

"Thank you."

Abel was aware that he had a spring in his step, and he didn't care. He didn't care what people thought about him, not right now. He was on the moon, and he was going to stay there for a few more hours—although he doubted that the high of being married to Philip would ever entirely fade.

"That was quite a show."

Abel briefly closed his eyes. He didn't want to talk to Milton, the rodent alpha. He wasn't even sure why he was there or who had invited him. "Milton. Thank you for coming."

Milton shrugged. "I wasn't sure I should. It was a good show, though. Almost made me believe you actually like him."

Abel was *not* going to beat the shit out of Milton with the plate he was holding. "That's because I *do* love him. This is a marriage of love."

"And of convenience. I might not have been present at the last meeting, but I still know what happened and what's been decided. When is he going to the prickle?"

162

"I don't know. In a few days, I think."

"Maybe move that to tomorrow, eh? The sooner we deal with this, the better it will be for everyone."

"I don't doubt that, but as you might have noticed, today is my wedding day. I'd like to enjoy the evening with my husband and my son."

Milton raised his hands. "Of course. Sorry to disturb you, and congratulations."

Abel sighed. "Thank you." He hadn't meant to ruffle Milton's feathers. He needed Milton. They all did.

It was easy to forget all about Milton once Abel was back with Philip and Myron. Myron was fussy, no doubt tired, and watching Philip with him made Abel's heart feel like it had swollen. This was his family now.

"I can take him for the night again," Chris offered once the party was winding down. Myron wasn't asleep yet, and he hadn't left Philip's arms.

Philip bit his lower lip and looked at Abel. "I know we'd planned for it, but I don't like how fussy he is."

Abel kissed Philip's cheek. "You want to keep him for the night."

"Yes. If that's okay with you."

"Of course it is. He needs his dad. It's been a big day for him, too, even though he doesn't understand what happened." One day, Philip wouldn't be hesitant when it came to Abel and Myron. He'd understand that Abel had meant it when he'd said that he wanted to be Myron's father.

"I know this probably wasn't your idea of a honeymoon," Philip said as they walked upstairs. They were going to spend the night in Philip's room, and Abel was planning to stay a few more days there, too. Rod had promised to keep his absence quiet, so even though it wasn't exactly a honeymoon, it was something.

"My idea of a honeymoon is being with you," Abel told

him.

Philip gave him a sheepish smile. "I know that, but still. Honeymoons are for newlyweds to have fun."

"And this isn't?"

"I suppose it depends on what you think of as fun."

"Philip, *anything* I do with you is fun."

Philip laughed and pushed open the bedroom door. "I doubt changing diapers is enjoyable."

"You're right, it's not, but it's part of what I agreed to. It's part of what I *want*. Being with you isn't just about the fun times and the sex. It's also about taking care of you and Myron, being there for you both if you need it, and Myron needs it right now, so you're going to change him, then we're going to get into bed with him for a bit, try to calm him down enough for him to sleep."

Philip smiled. "You have everything planned."

"Not this, no. But I've spent enough time dreaming about being with you to know what I want—you and Myron, with everything that comes with it, the joys and the problems."

Philip leaned against Abel. "Thank you."

"What for?"

"Being here for me. Loving me. Loving Myron."

"That's never going to change, Philip. Whatever will happen tomorrow or the day after that, I'm not going anywhere. I need you to believe that."

"I do."

They were stronger together, maybe even strong enough to take down the rotting part of the council, the one that was trying to use their power to control the shifters in the forest.

CHAPTER THIRTEEN

Philip wanted to turn back and run home. He wanted to hide in the forest, possibly with Abel. He'd wanted to never come back there again—to never see the people who'd hurt him so much.

Yet there he was, on his way to the prickle, and he couldn't go back.

Abel was driving. He was looking straight ahead, but Philip knew he was aware of him and how uncomfortable he was. Abel always was. "I don't like this," he murmured.

"Well, we *can* go back if you don't want to do it," Abel suggested.

Philip sighed. "I know." But he didn't ask Abel to turn the car around. He couldn't. He might feel like he was about to throw up, and he might not want to do this, but he had to. For Myron, for his son's future, heck, for his and Abel's future. They needed to start their life as a married couple, but they were in limbo right now. Abel couldn't move in with Philip, and Philip couldn't leave the Bishop house. Even though he was married, he and Myron were safer there, at least until they knew what would happen with the council.

"I won't let anything happen to you. You're my husband, and no one has the right to touch you or take you away."

Philip snorted. "That doesn't mean they won't try."

"And that's why we're here," Jacob said from the backseat. He and Monroe had volunteered to come, and while Philip wasn't sure it was a good thing—it would look like they were expecting trouble or like Philip needed to be defended—he was grateful for their presence. He trusted Abel to keep him safe, but that didn't mean they couldn't do with four more hands, just in case. Philip wasn't sure what they'd find when they got to the prickle. If Beta Robertson had already managed to wiggle his ass into the alpha position, he might try to get Philip back and hurt Abel, and that was something Philip did *not* want to talk about.

"We're here," Abel said.

Philip swallowed, or at least he tried to, but his mouth was dry. "You need to stop there, at the little house. Someone's going to ask you who you are and what you're doing here."

Abel did what Philip had said, but no one was there.

It was weird—there had always been someone guarding the entrance to prickle territory before. Of course, Alpha Grimes had been the one who'd decided who had to do it, so maybe now that he was dead, everyone stayed away.

"What now?" Abel asked.

"Drive, I guess. The first house you'll see is the alpha's house. Everyone will probably be there." Unless the elders were meeting somewhere else, which wouldn't have surprised Philip. They were sneaky assholes.

No one tried to stop them, not even when they parked in front of the house and got out of the car. Philip looked around, but no one was there. They could hear voices coming from inside, though, so he was pretty sure they'd find who they were looking for.

Philip tried knocking at the door, but he doubted anyone heard him. He knocked again to be able to say he'd tried more than once, then he took a deep breath and opened the door.

The place hadn't changed. Philip hadn't been there often, but he still remembered the smell—wood and alcohol, sweat, furniture polish. It made him want to run away, but instead, he squared his shoulders and stepped in. "Hello? Anyone here?" he called out.

Abel, Jacob, and Monroe were right behind him. He could see how tense they were, ready to attack if anyone tried to hurt him.

A door opened. Abel grabbed Philip's hand, and Philip could have kissed him. He'd known he needed the reassurance even without him asking.

"Philip? Is that you?"

Philip swallowed. "It is." He recognized the voice. Marla was one of the good ones—if something like that existed in the prickle. She was one of the elders, and she'd always made Philip think about his grandmother. He'd never known her, but she'd been Marla's best friend.

"What are you doing here?" She bustled toward him, looking around. "You shouldn't be here. You were safe. Why did you come back?"

Abel cleared his throat. "We're here because Philip has a say in who the next alpha will be."

Marla blinked. "He does?"

Philip didn't want to talk about this, but there was no avoiding it. "My son does. *Oscar's* son. But he's only a few months old, so the task falls to me."

Marla's eyes widened. "Oscar's son?" She glared. "If that man weren't already dead, I'd wrap my hands around his neck and squeeze until he was dead. That—that fucking asshole."

Philip blinked. This wasn't the reaction he'd expected. "Marla?"

She waved. "I know. Sorry. But knowing Oscar and you, I don't believe for one second that you had his son because you wanted to. That's one of the reasons I was happy to find out you were gone. Alpha Grimes said you'd been kidnapped, but no one believed that. I was hoping you'd been saved." She looked down at Philip's hand. His fingers were linked with Abel's, and it was hard to miss the ring on his finger. "I hope it was your choice."

Philip squeezed Abel's hand. "It was. I've never been this happy."

"Good. Why did you come back, then? I know you have a say in the next alpha, but if it were me, I'd have left the bunch of us to rot after what we did to you."

"No matter how little I like to think of it, Oscar was Myron's biological father, and Myron is a porcupine shifter. I want him to be able to come here when he's older, if that's what he wants. These are his roots. I don't want him to come here to find Alpha Robertson, though. Things would only get worse."

Marla grinned. "Thank God you're here, then. We're at a standstill. Three for Robertson, three for Lindsay."

Philip gaped. "Some of you have chosen Lindsay?"

"Not everyone here is an old bitch. Yes, three of us want Lindsay to become the next alpha. The other three aren't okay with that, though. I'm sure you heard the yelling."

"We did."

"Come in, then. I'm not sure how the others are going to react, but you have guards, so they won't attack." She smiled. "And you're married."

Abel offered her his free hand. "Council Member Porter, ma'am."

"Oh, a council member. You did well, Philip."

She turned and walked back to what had been Alpha Grimes' office. When she opened the door, there was a moment of silence, from both sides. Philip took a deep breath and stepped in.

"Marla, where were you?" someone snarled.

"Didn't you hear someone was here? You're getting deaf, Daniel?"

"Who was it?" another voice asked.

It was so much, yet Philip had to face it. He couldn't go back, not now.

He held his head high and stepped farther into the office. The elders were sitting in front of Alpha Grimes' desk. Only the six of them were there, but Philip had no doubt that Beta Robertson and Lindsay were around. "Hello," he said.

Then he watched all hell break loose.

He couldn't hear much over the yelling, so he stayed still. He felt safe enough with Abel, Jacob, and Monroe there with him. The elders were, well, old, so they wouldn't attack— probably. Daniel did look like he might try to tear Philip's head off, though.

"What are you doing here?" he snarled, making Philip wonder if he was able to talk normally.

"I have a right to be here."

"You're a carrier. You have no rights."

Abel growled, and it was something Philip hadn't expected. "Philip is my husband."

Daniel didn't have to be told who Abel was. He paled and tilted his head forward. "Council Member Porter."

"Can you all shut up and listen to Philip now? He'll explain why we're here."

Philip was going to hate this. He waited for everyone to shut up, then started talking, carefully not looking at them. "Alpha Grimes allowed Oscar to take me from my home and rape me repeatedly. Oscar had me abort my first child because she was a girl. Then, when I was pregnant with my son, I was rescued."

"You can't talk about Alpha Grimes and Oscar this way!" Daniel yelled.

Jacob took a step forward. It was enough for the elder to snap his mouth shut.

Philip cleared his throat. "What happened in the past

doesn't matter. They're both dead. But as Oscar's biological son, Myron has a say in who the next alpha will be. Since he can't exercise that right, I will do it in his place."

Abel was so damn proud of Philip. He was facing the people who hadn't done anything to help him when he'd been raped and had his little girl taken away from him. Abel didn't think he'd ever met someone this brave.

"You can't vote," that Daniel asshole said. Two of the other elders nodded, although they didn't look as sure as he sounded.

Philip let go of Abel's hand. He crossed his arms over his chest. "Why not?"

"You're a carrier."

"And? That doesn't change the fact that Myron is my son. Mine, and Oscar's. Shouldn't he have the right to Oscar's legacy?"

"He's a newborn."

"That's why I, as his other father, will take his place. Isn't that how things work?"

"But—"

Abel cleared his throat. "I don't know how you people do things here, but as it is, Philip and Myron also stand to inherit everything Oscar left. Unless he was married and had other children?" Abel already knew the answer to that, but it was fun to watch the elders try to come up with something. He also knew Philip didn't want any of Oscar's things, and while Abel could understand that, he thought Philip could do some good with Oscar's money, both for the prickle and for the forest in general.

"He didn't," the woman who'd met them in the hallway said. "So yes, Myron will inherit everything. Including Oscar's right to have a say in how the prickle is run."

"I don't want a day-to-day say in it," Philip said. "I don't care what happens after this is over. But I *am* going to vote for Lindsay to be the next alpha."

That, of course, brought up a new series of yells and protests. Abel didn't miss the way three of the elders reacted, though. They were glad. They were satisfied. They were apparently going to have the support they'd needed to make this happen.

Abel and Philip were lucky they had the support of half the elders. This was going to be easier than they'd thought. Hopefully, it meant they could do it now, go home, and never come back. No matter how brave Philip was, Abel knew he was probably freaking out inside.

"I suggest we vote right now," he said.

"We can't do that," Daniel protested. Of course he did. He was always protesting against something or other.

"Why not? Everyone who is supposed to vote is here, right? All the elders?"

"They are, but—"

"We can send someone to fetch Lindsay Grimes and Beta Robertson once we've voted. They don't have a vote, so their absence doesn't matter."

"But . . ."

"He's right, Daniel," one of the other elders said. She was staring at Philip, and it was alarming, even though Abel knew she wouldn't try anything. Probably.

"Karen—"

Oh. That was Karen, the woman Philip thought would be a good council member. She'd tried to help Philip.

"No. He's right. The only people needed to vote on this are here. We don't have a new alpha yet because we were split between Lindsay and Beta Robertson. Since we now have a seventh voter, we won't be split anymore. The prickle needs an alpha and a council member."

171

"Ready for the vote, then?" Marla asked. She sounded too happy about this, but Abel wasn't worried.

There were a few grumbles, mostly from Daniel, but they were doing this.

"The choice is between Lindsay, Alpha Grimes' daughter, and Beta Robertson," he said.

He got a few nods. "All right. Raise your hand if you want Beta Robertson to become the prickle's next alpha."

Abel wasn't surprised to see three hands shoot up. He also wasn't surprised at Daniel's anger when he realized that wasn't going to be enough.

"Lindsay?" he asked.

Four hands rose. There was a moment of silence, and Abel could see Daniel and the other two elders who had voted with him wanted to protest. They couldn't, though. They'd voted, and they'd lost. Lindsay would be the new alpha if she agreed to it, and they could do nothing against that.

Abel didn't doubt that they'd try to influence Lindsay under the guise of helping her learn the job, and he hoped she'd see that and act accordingly. Philip seemed to think she could make this work. Karen apparently agreed with him, so hopefully, they'd manage. The council wouldn't have a say in how the prickle was led, though. Abel didn't want it to, but he and everyone else needed Karen to be the next council member for the prickle.

"We should call Lindsay and have her come here," Karen said. "She'll want to know what happened and to talk to Philip and Council Member Porter, since they're here. The rest of you can go. I'll stay here until Lindsay arrives and give her the news."

"We should all be there for that," Daniel started.

Karen cut him off. "In a normal situation, probably, but nothing about this is normal. I'm sure Lindsay will eventually talk to all of us, but there are more important things to do right now."

"Like giving that man Oscar's legacy?"

"Yes," Karen snapped. "We all know what happened, so don't act all high and mighty, Daniel. All of us, including you, knew that Oscar had taken Philip, with Alpha Grimes' approval. All of us knew he kept him somewhere and that his goal was to have a son from him. I wasn't surprised when Philip told us he'd been raped, or that Oscar was cruel enough to take his little girl from him. So let's stop acting like Oscar and Alpha Grimes weren't cruel men who used the power they had over all of us to get what they wanted, willing or not. The vote we just had is going to change things, for all of us, for the better. Unless you still think that what Alpha Grimes and Oscar did was right?"

Daniel avoided looking at her. "Fine. Call Lindsay. I still think this is a bad idea, but like you said, we voted. When she does something wrong and gets the prickle in danger, and she will, you'll regret it."

He got up and left, slamming the door behind himself. The other two elders who had voted with him followed suit, but Marla lingered. "They think she won't be able to do this because she's a woman." She snorted. "I'd like to see them try to do some of the things we have to deal with, but men have always been better at yapping their mouths and taking what they want rather than working for the community." She looked at Abel and Philip. "Present men excluded, of course. I'm glad you're okay, Philip, and that you found a good man. You deserve it after what you went through, and I'm sorry we couldn't do more for you. I wish we had, but you know how it was."

Philip nodded curtly. "I do."

He probably did, but that didn't mean he'd forgiven the prickle members, even if he understood why they hadn't done anything.

God, Abel couldn't wait to take Philip away from this place. He knew these people meant well, but they were hurting Philip. Being *there* was hurting him.

Marla left. They didn't have to wait long for Lindsay to arrive. Abel hadn't been sure what to expect, but it wasn't the gentle-looking woman who came in through the door. She paused as she walked into the office and looked around. "God, I hate this place," she murmured.

She was wearing jeans and a too-big sweater. Her blonde hair was loose around her round face, and her cheeks were dusted with freckles. She wasn't wearing any jewelry or make-up, and she looked young, younger than her forty-one years.

"Alpha Grimes," Karen said.

Lindsay shivered. "That doesn't sound good at all."

"You can refuse if you want."

"And let Robertson torture the prickle like my father did? I don't think so. I might not want to be an alpha, and I haven't been prepared to be one, but I won't back down. It's my duty."

Abel already liked her. He hadn't known her father, but from what she was saying, she'd be a better alpha than her father ever was.

Karen nodded. "Good. I didn't think you were going to refuse, but you can never know someone well enough. I'll leave the three of you to it. Philip and his husband probably have a lot to tell you, and they should have privacy to do so. You know where to find me if you need anything."

"Oh, I have no doubt I will." Lindsay eyed the chair behind the desk. "I need to buy a new chair." She sat on the edge of the desk instead. "So, Philip. Are you here to demand reparations for what Oscar and my father did to you?"

Philip was taken aback. "No. I don't want anything from the prickle. As far as I'm concerned, I'm not a member anymore. I belong with the deer now." He and Abel hadn't talked about it in details—too much was happening for them to find a moment to do it—but Philip knew they'd eventually move in with the herd. That was where Abel lived, where he belonged, so that was where Philip and Myron would go. Philip was happy about that. If he hadn't had that chance, he would have asked Thomas to make him and Myron cete members, even though they weren't badgers and they had no relationship to any of them except friendship.

Lindsay sighed. "I can't say I blame you. God knows I would have left a long time ago if I could have." She pinched the bridge of her nose. "All right. I know I have you to thank—or not—for my new position."

Philip grimaced. "I understand why you didn't want to be the alpha, but I think we made the right choice. The prickle needs someone good after, well . . ."

"After my father made a mess of things. You can say it. I know he was a cruel bastard. We fought about it often enough. I have the scars to show it." She looked at him. "I know we should have done more for you as a prickle, but I had my kids to think of. They'll always come first. I'm sure you understand that."

"I do." That was why Philip forgave her. He couldn't say the same about his own parents, though.

"Good. You'll always be welcome here, and I *will* do what I can to give you reparations."

"I don't need that."

"Maybe not, but it doesn't mean you shouldn't have it. This is one step toward changing the prickle for good. We need to pay for what happened. There are no two ways about it."

Philip could accept that. He wanted the prickle to get better, to become healthy and to leave Oscar and Alpha Grimes behind. He might not plan on living there ever again, but that didn't mean he wanted the people who did to have a bad life. "Thank you."

Lindsay nodded. "Now. I'm sure you're not here just to make sure I become the alpha."

That wasn't Philip's area, so he let Abel speak. He'd never been far, not since they'd left Bishop house. Philip was grateful for his presence. He knew he could have done this on his own—he was strong enough, no matter what he'd thought in the past—but knowing he had support had helped. It still did.

"I'm sure you know what's going on with the council," Abel said.

"Who doesn't?"

"We're split up, very much like your elders were. Some of us want to change the rules that are in place right now, especially regarding the carriers. They're men, just like I am, and they shouldn't be treated like commodities and traded by the council just because they think they have the power to do it."

"My father certainly thought that, as did Oscar. So you need my help to, what? Strike that rule down?"

"Yes and no. Look, I'm sure you know how important the person you choose will be. They'll uphold the prickle's rights with the council, and they can change the life of many people who aren't treated right by the council and their own alphas right now. We just want someone who will do the right thing, unlike Oscar."

"You have a name in mind."

It wasn't a question. She'd come prepared, and Philip was impressed.

"When we realized we needed the prickle to choose

someone on our side, we asked Philip who he thought would be a good choice."

"I see."

"He named Karen."

Lindsay looked at Philip. He wanted to hide, but he stayed right where he was. She might not be happy because he'd chosen someone before she'd become alpha, but that didn't mean it was the wrong choice. It wasn't like he'd made Karen the next council member anyway. He'd just suggested she might be a good selection, that was all.

"She's not a bad choice," Karen said.

"That's good to hear."

"I need to think about this, though. It will be my first decision as an alpha, and I have to get it right. I also want to make sure you know that whoever I pick, I won't allow it to be someone you and the rest of the council will be able to manipulate."

"That's not what we want. None of us will force anyone into making choices they don't approve. But something had to change. You know how Philip was treated. You know what he went through. I don't want anything like this to happen to anyone in the forest again, and neither should you. That means we need someone with a soul and a sense of what's right and wrong on the council. Whoever you choose, we only want that person to vote following their conscience, just like you will lead the prickle that way."

Lindsay huffed a laugh. "All right, I get it. And you're not wrong. I hate what was allowed to happen in the prickle, and I don't want it to happen to anyone else." She hesitated. "I think my son might be a carrier."

Philip's eyes widened. "He is?" If he remembered right, the boy was still young.

"Maybe. I was afraid of asking our healer to check him until now. Who knows what my father would have done with that knowledge? Probably sold him off to arrange something for the prickle. I didn't want that to happen, and I don't want anything like what was done to you to happen to him, either. I don't want to hand him off to the council and never see him again. So don't worry. Whoever I choose, they're going to work *for* people, not against them. They're not going to use them as pawns, not if I have anything to say about it."

Abel nodded.

Philip was relieved. He'd known he might not be doing the right thing by helping to get Lindsay elected as the next alpha, but now that he'd heard her talk, he didn't think he had. She wasn't like her father, and he hoped she'd show everyone that. The prickle had a good chance to make it out of this stronger.

"What do you think?" Abel asked as they left the house.

Philip was glad to leave it behind. He didn't want to come back. It held too many bad memories for him. "She sounds like a good person."

"She does. And I like that she's making us wait. It means she wants to think everything over before naming the next council member, and that's what the prickle needs." He stopped and faced Philip. "How are you? Really. Don't try to lie to me, because I'll know."

Philip had to smile at that. "I'm okay. I'll feel better once we're back home, though." He needed to see Myron. He knew his son was safe, but he couldn't deny he was shaken.

"We both will. And you don't have to come back."

Philip looked around. "Maybe I will." Not soon, but once Lindsay'd had enough time to work on the prickle, to make them see what they'd done wrong and to make it better, he might. This was the place where he was born, and he belonged there as much as his son did.

They also belonged with Abel and the deer now, though.

And *that* was where Philip would spend the rest of his life.

EPILOGUE

A bel blew a raspberry on Myron's stomach, delighted to hear him laugh. It had become their thing — to everyone's surprise, Abel loved to play with Myron, much more than Philip did. Philip enjoyed it, too, of course, but he didn't find it as fun as Abel did. Maybe it was because Abel didn't spend as much time with Myron, or because Philip still insisted on being the one to get up during the night if Myron needed it. It didn't matter, though. Abel had found his place with Myron. He was the fun dad.

He blew another raspberry and smiled at Myron tried to grab his hair. "We need to get you back into your clothes. Your daddy is going to have my ass if he finds you half-naked when he comes back."

"His daddy has already come back," Philip said from behind them. "You two are lucky you're cute."

Abel batted his lashes. "You'd love us even if we weren't."

Philip laughed, and it was the most gorgeous sound in the world. "You're right, I would. Are you ready to come downstairs for dinner?"

"Let me put on his socks, and we'll be."

Abel was spending most of his nights at the Bishop house now. The only times he stayed at home was when he needed to be in Northwood for council meetings. He knew it might be dangerous, but he couldn't stay away. He'd tried.

He hoped that now that Lindsay was officially the new prickle alpha, things would go better. She still hadn't chosen

180

a council member, but she needed to, and Abel thought she would make the right choice. In the meantime, he and Philip weren't going anywhere. Philip could have moved in with the herd since they were married, but Abel hadn't pushed. Philip had his friends at the Bishop house. They were his new family, and he needed them. There would be enough time to introduce him and Myron to the herd later, once things in the forest calmed down. In the meantime, Philip was happy, and that was all that mattered.

"Took you long enough," Chris teased Abel when he and Myron got downstairs.

"I'm not as fast as Philip at changing him, especially when he decides to wee while I'm putting on the clean diaper."

Chris laughed. "That's happened a few times," he said, waving around his fork.

Abel settled at the table next to Philip. Myron was still in his arms, but he didn't mind eating with one hand. It wasn't like he'd never done it. "I was lucky I managed to use the diaper as a shield."

"You were. The last time it happened to me, I had to shower by the time he was done." Chris' smile widened. "But it's good exercise, isn't it?"

"What for? I don't usually have people peeing on me."

"I meant for your next baby. When are you going to get that bun in Philip's oven?"

Philip's cheeks flushed. "Chris! You can't say that kind of thing over dinner!"

"Why not? Everyone here is wondering the same thing."

Abel shook his head. Philip's friends were great, but they were also nosy. "There's no rush. Myron is only four months old. We can wait a year or two to make him a big brother."

Chris pouted. "Aww. I wanted another baby in the house."

"Then maybe you and Jacob should start talking."

Chris gaped. "Abel!" He threw Abel his fork. Luckily, he didn't put a lot of force into it, and it landed on the table before reaching him. "You can't stay stuff like that."

"Why not? You just asked Philip and me when we were going to try for another baby. You're sticking your nose into our business, so I'm going to do the same with yours."

That knocked the wind right out of Chris' sails. Abel knew he was young, maybe too young to have a child, especially with Jacob. From what Abel knew, they still hadn't solved their problem, and maybe they never would. He hoped that getting rid of the carrier laws would help, though. At the very least, the carriers would eventually be able to go home instead of having to stay at the Bishop house. It would make things easier on everyone, and the distance might make Chris and Jacob realize they wanted to be together — or not.

"We could have a baby," Philip murmured, leaning closer to Abel.

"We could, but why rush? Aren't you happy?"

Philip bit his lower lip. "Of course I am. I was just wondering if maybe you didn't want a child that's yours, you know. So we can be a real family. A blood family."

"I already have a child who's mine, and the fact that we don't share blood doesn't matter. We're a family of the heart." Abel didn't have to add anything. He'd already told Philip he considered Myron his, and that wasn't going to change. He didn't even care if they didn't have other children. That was why he'd married Philip. He'd married him because he loved him, and he'd never cared about what Philip was and what he could give him, not beyond love and happiness.

Abel kissed Philip's cheek. "We *can* have another baby if you're ready, although I think I'd rather wait until this little one stops waking up at night. I don't know how we'd manage if we had two of them crying at two AM."

Philip grimaced. "True. And maybe it would be better to wait until I can move in with you and the forest is calmer again."

"It would be." Although that wouldn't stop them if they *were* ready for another baby. But Myron was still so young, and Abel wanted to dedicate himself to him before adding to their family.

Abel's phone rang in his pocket. He juggled Myron until Philip rolled his eyes and took him. Abel smiled gratefully and answered. "Yes."

"We have a new council member," Calder said.

"We do?"

"Yep. We have a meeting tomorrow to meet her."

Abel leaned back in his chair. "Her?"

"You already know who it is. You orchestrated all of this perfectly."

"So Lindsay did select Karen?" That got a few people's attention, including Philip's, whose eyes widened slightly.

"She did. Karen called the office to tell them about it and request the stuff she'll need and the documents."

"That's good." It was going to take a little while to get everything settled, but this was a huge step forward.

"Damn right it is. We have a fighting chance now."

"You know things aren't going to be easy." The council members who wanted to stay in the past were going to fight this every step of the way, and the alphas were going to be worse. There was no guarantee that they'd follow the laws, and since the council had no say in how they led their people, it would be next to impossible to police them. But the carriers were a vulnerable group, and they were going to fight tooth and nail for their lives to get better. Abel wasn't going to let anyone treat a carrier the way Philip had been treated, even if it cost him his spot as a council member.

He didn't care about the job, not any further than the possibilities it gave him to make people's lives better. He had everything he could ever want in life waiting for him at home, so even without the job, he'd be happy.

He already was.

YOU MAY ALSO ENJOY THE FOLLOWING FROM EXTASY BOOKS INC:

Michael
Catherine Lievens

Excerpt

Cooper wiggled out of the window. He plastered his back against the wall and slid sideways, keeping his focus on his feet until he reached the edge of the roof. Then he turned, pressed one hand on the roof next to the trellis, and turned around. The trellis shook with every move he made, but he got to the ground safely, just like he always did when he snuck out of the house.

He pushed his hair away from his face and looked around, just in case, even though he knew people only rarely left the house. That was mostly because Alpha Carter had forbidden it, but Cooper was the only one who'd spent much time in the garden even before that.

He frowned at the state of his flowers. They were all dead by now, suffocated by wild grass and lack of care. He made his way on what had once been a path but was now little more than an overgrown graveled area and moved away from the house.

This was why he'd always enjoyed the garden. It was big,

but not too big, and he'd found the hidden place when he was a kid and still allowed to run around. There hadn't been much to it back then, but he'd worked on it while he'd still been able to, and now it was a perfect hiding place.

It was tucked away to the side, near the fence that ran along the entire perimeter of pride territory. The trees and bushes were plentiful there, and Cooper had installed a small bench between them. The vegetation hid it, and the only way to see it was to walk in front of it. These days, he encouraged the bushes to grow in front of it. He hoped it would create a small enclave where he could spend time hiding from the world, or at least, from his world.

He didn't want to hide from what was outside the fence, but from what was inside of it.

He pushed the bushes to the side and slid onto the bench. The bushes didn't cover the entire bench, so Cooper made sure to move to the side that wasn't visible. He doubted anyone had noticed him leaving the house, or even that anyone had decided to do the same and sneak out. He knew other pride members didn't like what Alpha Carter was doing, but most of those who had a problem with him had slowly trickled out over the years, like Lenny and Scott. They were free now, and Cooper sometimes wondered if living in the forest in his tiger form wouldn't be better than the daily beatings he took.

He knew it would be.

He was inching closer and closer to making that decision and changing his life. He wasn't sure what held him back, but it was probably fear. He didn't care about leaving his parents behind—they'd never tried to defend him from Alpha Carter, and he didn't think they ever would. He didn't have siblings, something that made Alpha Carter angry with his family. No, Cooper wouldn't regret anything he'd leave behind.

But he was afraid. He was terrified. He had no way of knowing what he'd find when he left the pride. As bad as living there was, as much as he hated Alpha Carter and everyone else in the pride for not taking a stand against him, it was his home, and all he knew. Not being able to tell what would happen to him once he left it was what held him back, but he'd get over it soon. He knew it.

He sighed. He loved spending time outside, but he could never stay long, not when Alpha Carter might need him. The man wasn't predictable except in the way he'd make Cooper pay if he didn't find him when he needed him or when Cooper did something he didn't like. That happened all too often, and it was Cooper's fault. If only he could keep his mouth shut. But sometimes, the words got out of his mouth without him even thinking about it.

He got up and brushed his ass off. He looked around, and when he was satisfied he was alone, he snuck back to the house. He managed to get all the way to the trellis before getting caught, and he was glad he hadn't started climbing it, because that would have been a dead giveaway of how he'd left the house.

"What are you doing outside?" Beta Boyd asked, his voice harsh and cold. He was as bad as Alpha Carter, so Cooper didn't even try to mollify him.

"I wanted to check the flowers."

Beta Boyd snorted. "They've been dead for a long time."

"I couldn't have known that, since I haven't been allowed to leave the house in a long time."

Beta Boyd's eyes blazed with anger. "Mouthy, aren't you? Well, it's nothing Alpha Carter can't deal with." He grabbed Cooper's arm and dragged him toward the front door.

Cooper didn't protest and didn't try to fight his hold even though it hurt. It was nothing next to what awaited him, and it would only make Alpha Carter and Beta Boyd angrier.

Beta Boyd pulled Cooper into the house and toward Alpha Carter's office. He knocked, waited until the alpha told him to open, and pushed Cooper through before following him into the room.

"What's going on?" Alpha Carter asked.

He was sitting behind his desk, and Cooper wondered if he was actually working or if he was watching porn. Since he'd caught the alpha masturbating in his office more than once, he wouldn't be surprised at either of those options. He looked dressed, though, so he'd probably been working. Cooper wasn't sure which interruption was worse in the alpha's eyes, but either way, he knew a beating was coming his way. Hopefully, Alpha Carter wouldn't break anything this time.

"I found him in the garden," Beta Boyd said. Cooper glared at him.

"In the garden, huh? What were you doing out there, Cooper?"

Cooper sighed. Not answering would only make things worse. "I was checking the flowers."

"The flowers?"

"Yes. I like being in the garden and tending to them."

"Yet you're forbidden from leaving the house. How did you get out?"

There was no way Cooper was telling them about it. His bedroom window was supposed to be locked, and it had been once. But Cooper had managed to break the lock, even though looking at it, you couldn't tell. "The back door. There was no one in the kitchen, and I snuck out. I just wanted to see the flowers."

Alpha Carter rose from his chair, and Cooper steeled himself. He saw the backhand coming, and even though he was expecting it, it didn't help him stay upright. He stumbled back and knocked against Beta Boyd. The man growled and pushed Cooper forward.

Cooper never knew if it was better to face the beatings on his feet or on the floor. He almost always started on his feet, but would his not falling make the alpha even angrier? The man liked being bowed to, having the visual that he was the better, more powerful man.

Cooper slid to his knees, ignoring the throbbing in his cheek.

The second hit made his head snap back. At least it was on the other cheek, although considering how much it hurt, maybe it wasn't a good thing. Cooper didn't know. He just wanted this to be over so he could go lick his wounds in his bedroom.

He was grateful and relieved when Alpha Carter ordered Beta Boyd to take him to his room and lock him in. It meant he wouldn't get lunch, and probably not even dinner, but he'd be able to tend to his wounds, curl in his bed, and rest.

This nightmare would be there when he woke up tomorrow morning, and the day after that, until he finally found the courage to leave. Every punch, every slap, was a step toward that decision. Cooper was going to have to make it before things got too bad, though. He wasn't sure why, but Alpha Carter was becoming more violent, especially with him.

If he didn't leave, he was probably going to die under the alpha's hands, and no one would care. How sad was that?

About the Author

Catherine lives in Italy, country of good food and hot men. She used to write fantasy as a child, but it was reading her first gay erotic romance novel that made her realize that that was what she really wanted to write.

After graduating from college in English language and translation, she divides her day between writing, reading, taking care of her son and reading some more.

You can find her on Facebook and Twitter or on her website: authorcatherinelievens.wordpress.com

Email: lievens.catherine@gmail.com

Newsletter: http://eepurl.com/c-uvKn

www.ingramcontent.com/pod-product-compliance
Lightning Source LLC
Chambersburg PA
CBHW060813120626
46557CB00001B/197